OTHER TITLES BY RAVEN OAK

Amaskan's Blood (Boahim Series)
The Eldest Silence (Xersian Series)*

* *forthcoming by Grey Sun Press*

PRAISE FOR *AMASKAN'S BLOOD*

"With a ferocious-yet-fragile heroine, resonant themes, and a sweepingly gorgeous backdrop, *Amaskan's Blood* delivers food for thought *and* frank enjoyment."
Maia Chance, author of the Fairy Tale Fatal series

"An exciting epic fantasy filled with intrigue and layers upon layers of well crafted secrets and lies."
Stephanie Hildreth of *100 Pages a Day*

"…a story that is like the love child of Bujold's Paladin of Souls and Patricia Brigg's Masques…If you enjoy intrigue, religions and politics this would be a good match for you."
LibraryThing Early Reviews

"Holy crap, this is good!"
Seattle Geekly

"We all enjoyed her book immensely….*Amaskan's Blood* most certainly receive[s] the Sparkle Motion stamp of approval."
Sparkle Motion Book Club

"[A] fantasy novel in its truest form…these well-developed individuals held me captive. It was a very strong start to a fantasy series that I very much look forward to following."
Pure Jonal: Confessions of a Bibliophile

CLASS-M EXILE

RAVEN OAK

Geek Girl Con 2019

Welcome to Bay-zar!

CLASS-M EXILE

RAVEN OAK

GREY SUN
— PRESS —

Grey Sun Press
PO Box 1635
Bothell, WA 98041
WWW.GREYSUNPRESS.COM

ISBN 978-0-9908157-4-7

Library of Congress Control Number: 2015936484

This novella was an experiment and an accident, one dedicated to all the oddballs in school who thought they didn't matter & that the bullying would never stop.
You were stronger than you knew.

And knowing you gave me strength, too.

1

A Fish without a Bicycle

Bay-zar.

Class-M planet in the middle of no-where. Dust, dust, and more dust. Unless ya circled 'round to the more habitable region, you'd be stuck without a ship to anywhere. 'Round the corner though, you could find everything from ship parts and dried food packs, to roast dog and the rare *bi-cycle*. Hell, you could even buy yourself a *gen-u-ine* religion if you were so inclined.

I wasn't sure why I'd come here; touristin' weren't my thing. Only that I'd never been to Bay-zar, and everyone said ya hafta visit at least once. It wasn't the humidity that left my noses crinklin' in the bright sun, but the smell of manure and too many beings as hundreds of heads bobbed up and down in a sea of booths, goods, and tourists.

The ultimate tourist trap. And here I'd taken the bait.

Sweat pooled inside my heavy ship boots. Other tourists from the ship bumped ma elbows as they disembarked *The Marzipan* (don't ask, the captain has weird taste in food, or so I heard). This little squirt elbowed his way past me and half-a-dozen folks crowded 'round a blazin' red booth promisin' trinkets made of *gen-u-ine* gold, fresh from the mines of *Miral*.

I cringed when he hollered 'bout his silly ideas for usin' dead folks for energy. I weren't but three steps away from this fool when a white-hooded figure shoved its way through the crowd.

She skidded to a stop just inside my personal space. "Ever been to Bay-zar?" she asked with a quick glance over her shoulder. Two beefy men carryin' scowls were comin' in fast 'nough to knock over a stand of leafy green somethin's. Girl leaned close to me like we was kin, and my frame hid her as them military beefcakes passed.

Every race, religion, creed, gender, species, and nationality in over a hundred worlds traveled through Bay-zar, or so I'd heard, but never before had I seen her kind outside a book. Hell, I didn't think they even existed no-more.

A departin' shuttle sent a cloud of dust skitterin' 'cross us, and her hood fell back. Whispers moved 'cross the market like rain—first as tiny droplets, mostly ignored 'til the downpour caught everyone off guard. Then all motion stopped. The market's chatterin' and clankin' died as all focus shifted to her. One of them fancy gentleman tumbled over a child in his attempt to flee. Some three-eyed creature let loose a half-cough, half-scream as it raced up the ramp of *The Marzipan*.

"What?" I asked. "She's just a *hu*-man."

"B-but look at her! She's only got two eyes!" a voice cried out.

"Yeah, and two legs. Who uses two legs anymore?"

The cries from them tourists continued, but the female *hu*-man stood there in cargo pants and a tee-shirt that read, "A woman without a man is like a fish without a bicycle."

To them, she was the plague. She was a one-way trip into the flames of a dyin' sun.

And she was awesome.

I didn't know what a fish was, and I'd never seen a real *bi*-cycle, but by golly, I was gonna find out.

"The name's Eerl." Somewhere in all my readin', I recalled somethin' 'bout hands bein' important to *hu*-mans. I held a slightly damp hand palm-up in front of her face. When she exposed two rows of lightly yellowed teeth, someone behind us growled as they passed. But she kept on a-smilin' and flashin' those weapons like they weren't nothin' at all.

"Mel." She seized my hand and pumped it up and down. "You've never been to Bay-zar?"

I shook my head. "Nope. First time. You?"

"I live here. Sort of." Another growl as a *Rharstian* passed, his tentacled eyes dartin' back and forth. 'Round us, tourists settled back into their hagglin' over knick-knacks and patti-macks, whatever *they* were. I ain't sayin' folks huddled near or nothin'; in fact, a nice empty circle settled 'round us.

"I ain't never heard of *hu*-mans livin' here. Once upon a time maybe, but—"

Her laughter cut like them hydraulics on the *The Marzipan* when they went belly up, but I pretended not to notice. "Where do you think that phrase came from?" she asked, and I shrugged. More laughter from her sent a whiff of moldy bread my way.

With breath like that, no wonder them folks were scared, but I reckoned it were more 'n that. A quick look-see showed her body to be little more than bones and whipcord. She went on like she never noticed my frown. "From humans. More than half of your Common vocabulary came from Earth. Hell, your accent would put you right at home in the southern United States…."

More words I ain't never heard. What were *states* and how'd they get all united? I mean, there was a war goin' on. As far as I knew, Earth was dead, long destroyed by them damned *ryddarl*—nothin' more than bottom feeders from Ryddar with enough firepower to blow up a sun and then some. When she said *home*, I lost what little there was to my river of thought.

"…But I figure it's somewhere out there."

"What is?" I asked.

Her smile sorta fell gentle-like. Poor girl weren't nothin' more than a youngin' standin' two footed on the dirt of Bay-zar. Poor and alone. My heart sank.

"My home. Earth," she said and fingered the stone slung 'round her neck with a frayin' rope.

"That's it!" The shout from behind weren't nothin' compared to the shove that came next as a beefy, red-skinned man with a taser grabbed her tee-shirt. "You aren't welcome here! You've been told that before, human. Now get gone." He glared and twirled the taser by the wrist strap with one finger.

"But she lives here," I muttered, and the muscles of his four arms thickened.

Before I had a chance of findin' out exactly what that meant, a deep rumble set the booths to tremblin' and the market's chatter returned to silence. Mel's blue eyes widened, and she whispered, "Oh, damn." She didn't laugh no-more, didn't smile neither. Just stood transfixed. Mel stared at the sky like the heavens were fallin', even when the red-skinned enforcer jabbed her shoulder with his meaty fingers. I followed her gaze, as did the rest of them folks in the market. And when the shadow fell 'cross us, blottin' out the sun, even the enforcer fell silent.

It was *big*.

Well, big didn't do it justice, but I'm a simple *Tersic*—words weren't ever my strength. Damned *ryddarl* ship blackened that sky and then groaned under the weight of its own size. I ain't never seen a ship like that. *The Marzipan* coulda fit in that ship's pocket, and ya would've never seen it in all the coils and loops and doo-dads hangin' from the engines of that behemoth.

If you've seen a herd of cattle escapin' a cyber-lion, you've seen Bay-zar in that moment. Feet kickin' up dust as people ran in every direction, though none was the right one. Didn't matter if they went left or right, that ship was everywhere. Mel trembled beside me. Those eyes—only two of 'em, yet I'd swear she seen more than me when she done looked at the underbelly of that ship.

One moment she was still. The next, she gave me a shove that done sent me outta the street and behind some flimsy curtain. I had just enough time to recognize it as a street vendor's booth before Mel barreled in. "Keep moving!" she shouted.

I didn't know where we was goin', but I reckoned I didn't need to. The screams and groans outside hurt my ears, and Mel gave my hand a desperate tug. The youngin' led me through a maze of booths and back alleys that smelled of piss and shit. So strong was the smell, bile rose in my throat. That ship landed

11

somewhere behind us, and silence descended. We musta run circles 'cause I saw *The Marzipan* as we ducked behind an empty wooden crate.

Several smaller ships burned. Somethin' struck *The Marzipan* with a muffled thud, but the shields held. I'll admit, I didn't do much thinkin'. My brain spun 'round in all that chaos while bodies dropped to the dust below. As Mel tried to catch her wind, I hauled her over to *The Marzipan* and pushed her through the open hatch. "What are you doing?" she hissed, but I shushed her. No need to call attention to her or nothin'. I tossed her jacket's hood over her head to cover them dark-brown curls and placed a finger to her lips.

"Don't say nothin'."

The hatch closed behind us, cuttin' off the sun. All them practice drills paid off as I pulled Mel toward the cargo hold's front. Slightly muted sobs dead ahead corrected my path when I turned wrong, and soon after, the beam from a flashlight hit my front eyes. The light shifted to Mel's hood-covered face before it clicked off, strandin' us in darkness.

"Why are the lights out?" someone whispered.

"The shields are taking too much power, I suppose."

The speaker was hushed by one of *The Marzipan*'s guards who asked, "Everyone here?"

"Everyone except Rhiohl. He's dead."

I didn't know which one of the passengers said it. Didn't rightly recall who Rhiohl was either. Guess it didn't matter no-more.

When a crew-member ordered us strapped into the racks, I took care of Mel. Weren't no reason to alert anyone—not yet anyway. She stayed quiet-like as she leaned against the cushioned wall-rack. When the belt clicked 'cross her scraggly frame and locked her into

12

place, I seen the fear in her eyes just the once before she blinked it away. Sharpness stared back as I belted myself in. She took holda my hand and squeezed.

The Marzipan's thrusters sent a vibration through my feet. We were leavin' Bay-zar.

If we were lucky, we'd make it off world alive. And if we were luckier, no one would notice the *hu*-man stowaway.

2

Out the Airlock

The mystery of our escape from the *ryddarl* kept me frettin' on it rather than worryin' on the folks 'round me on *The Marzipan*. Mel kept her head down as the ship shuddered and bucked its way through Bay-zar's atmo. A couple a dips set my stomach turnin' and my ears to poppin'. Weren't but a quiet few minutes 'til the ship's artificial grav kicked in. The lights remained dim for a mite before brightenin'. We were free and into the deep.

One moment, we were ace. The next, these two sisters from Barduun II did the math on Mel's appendages.

The scream they let loose made my ears wanna curl up and die. You'd've thought Mel was a *ryddarl* herself the way the captain glared, but I planted my three feet in front of Mel and glared right back.

"She has to go!"

"She's an albatross."

15

Both sisters talked right over each other. I done rolled my eyes at the silly little fools. "Barta, Marta, do ya even know what that word means? I don't think it means what ya think. Besides, where'd ya learn an Earth word like that?"

"Like you're one to talk," muttered Marta.

"What word?" asked Barta.

"Albatross," Mel whispered. The way she sorta shrank in on herself, I reckoned it weren't the first time she'd been called somethin' cruel. The crowd pressed closer to us, and I puffed out my chest, though the unicorn on my shirt might've diminished my false bravado a tad.

"She's cursed. I know that word. She'll bring the *ryddarl* back!" This was from a little squirt who'd "accidentally" bumped into me as he'd deboarded *The Marzipan*. His apology was as shitty as his lame-brained ideas 'bout human fuel.

Marta shouted, "Put her out the airlock!"

"What if *she* brought the attack?" The little squirt scratched his nose as he tried to hide compound eyes behind red-rimmed eyelids.

"Yeah! She's human! They're all violent creatures. War makers!"

"And how do ya know that?" I asked.

Barta's nose scrunched up. "Every war that's ever been was started by those humans. Everyone knows *that*."

The whines set my nerves a-janglin' and when this tough-guy type stuck his face in mine, the rot on his breath was more violent than anything I'd ever done. The look in his eyes—not sane at all. "You can't just kill her!" I shouted over all them voices, but they went right on with their crazy talk.

"Out with her!"

"But she'll die. Captain, ya can't seriously—"

"Who cares if she dies? Didn't her kind kill yours at the beginning of the war?"

Mel cocked her head to the side as she stared at me. She couldn't figger it—that much was clear. Honestly, I couldn't figger it myself. Why was I defendin' her? Them folks be right that her kind's war had brought all sorta trouble to my own. I flushed hot at the thought, but my eyes fell to Mel's shirt. Them folks didn't want her gone for nothin' other than fear. I weren't gonna let 'em kill her, not when I had so many questions. I stood taller, starin' right into the face of that beefcake. There was no way I'd win in a throwdown with someone almost twice my girth and muscle mass, but I was hopin' I wouldn't hafta.

I'd heard tales of a man named Moses partin' some red sea—he must've been vacationin' on Tyrus IV—but I never thought it possible. When Mel stepped between us, she parted the sea of passengers and crew just like that Moses fella. Them folks fell back a few steps, and the two sisters moaned.

Mel smiled like nothin' was wrong. "It's okay," she whispered to me as she rested a hand on my shoulder.

"Captain, ya can't do this. It's wrong, and ya done know it," I said, and he scowled. "Besides, I gotta know some things before I'm willin' to lay down and kill someone."

The lights went out. A clamor of screams and moans bounced 'round in my ears alongside *The Marzipan's* thrusters. Somethin' large hit the ship's side, and I clung to the racks with them others as unsecured crates slid 'cross the cargo hold. "Grav's malfunctioning, Captain," the pilot said over the communit.

"We should have never chartered with *The Marzipan*," Marta whispered to her sister.

17

The captain leaned his shiny, bald head against the wall's steel panelin' and sighed. "Look, Eerl, I know you like the human, but those are *ryddarl* on our tail. Would you kill us all?"

Barta wrapped her thick arms 'round her sister. The only thing separatin' them from bein' as bipedal as Mel was the mech tails they'd had implanted. That and the color of their skin. I didn't get the hatred one bit.

"Maybe if we turn her over to the *ryddarl*, they'll let us go!" said Marta.

Mel frowned. "You really think so? Do you know how many times the *ryddarl* have attacked Bay-zar in the past five years? Over a dozen. They didn't care that I was there. They didn't take me and leave the rest of you tourists to carry on. They just continued their slaughter without any regard for what planet one was born on. The only reason *The Marzipan* hasn't been blown sky-high is because the ship's too valuable in one piece."

Girl was right on the moolah. "Would ya hand over yer child? Yer sister, Marta, if it would save us all?" When I asked the question, Marta slapped me. The monster rock on her finger stung my jaw.

The Marzipan swayed as another volley of somethin' hit us. Mel's bottom lip slid out in a pout and trembled. "I just want to go home."

It must've been the glum way the words tumbled out,'cause them passengers quit their bitchin'. This passenger beside me coulda been anyone's granny— curly grey hair, three eyes whose color was faded just a touch, and stooped posture—she peered at Mel from 'round the beefcake. "She's just a child. Almost a baby, really." The sisters scowled, but granny paid 'em no mind. "Not her fault the *ryddarl* came to Bay-zar. She wasn't even grown when the war came."

The captain picked up the comm-unit. "*Ryddarl* still on our tail?"

"Negative. Another ship caught their eye."

The captain grunted. "Thom, get us out of here. Head for the nearest port—we've got some 'cargo' we need to dump."

And that was the end of it.

Mel wasn't bein' sent to her death right then, but it looked like she'd be departin' at the closest port. A few passengers mumbled, but no one was willin' to go against the captain and lose their credits.

"Everyone needs to remain in their rooms until we get clear of the *ryddarl*," the captain ordered. The crew split, but them passengers stood 'round gawkin'. They didn't wanna go first, their backs to the *hu*-man, but they weren't 'bout to leave her alone.

When the captain barked his orders a second time, I grabbed Mel by the elbow. "Let's get outta here."

"I don't have a room to go to."

I shook my head and propelled her forward. "You owe me credits, *Tersic*, for her ride," the captain called out behind us. Them passengers behind us came a smidge too close to clippin' my heels in their attempt to follow, and the rot smell on the tough guy's breath followed me clear down that narrow corridor. The captain's comm-unit squawked. Pilot was a-panickin' again, and the captain brushed past us in a rush. Left alone without him, the mutters swelled, and I picked up the pace. My three legs moved a lot faster than Mel's two. She jogged beside me to keep up.

When we reached the passenger quarters, I slid my ident card 'cross the lit panel lickety-split. The door slid open with more-than-a-hint of stale ship air. I didn't give her a moment's warnin' neither as I shoved her inside my room and sealed the door lock with a four-fingered handprint.

"You can't hide forever, human!" someone shouted as they passed. The ship pitched to the side, and passengers scurried like Bay-zarian rodents to their quarters.

After a minute or three, the corridor grew quiet-like. The eyes on the back of my head watched Mel. "Bet most of 'em be in their rooms now, hidin' 'til the *ryddarl* are gone. Are ya hungry? Thirsty?" I asked, and her stomach rumbled audibly. "When's the last time ya ate?"

Mel shrugged. "Sometime yesterday, I think. Had to steal some fruit from a vendor last night."

"You got no money?"

Another shrug. I tugged her by the arm. "Come on."

"Where are we going?"

Instead of answerin', I pulled her back through the door and along the now empty corridor to a dead end. A door slid open to the ship's mess hall: the ship's belly was laid out in an octagon shape and stuffed to the brim with long tables and stools, each one bolted to the floor. Only a brave few lingered while *The Marzipan* sent stomachs turnin' with the hard flyin'. I noted that none of 'em ate a thing. Conversations stopped as I pushed Mel along toward the food machine.

"I told you, I've got no money," she said.

I swiped my ident card. "Pick out somethin' to eat. I ain't havin' ya starve after I worked so hard to save ya and all."

Folks behind us whispered. Seemed like they was destined to follow us, especially if I was gonna make Mel a project of sorts. All that research I done on Earth, and here I was with a *gen-u-ine hu*-man. Maybe I could get some answers—assumin' I didn't end up at the end of someone's fork.

If I were lucky, that's how things would remain—whispers and accusations followin' us. If I weren't, like

20

I said—fork. *The Marzipan* settled a bit, and Mel scrolled through the screen.

She ordered a cheap Barlzen soup. Weren't nothin' but thin gruel. "Ya don't want something more…fillin'?"

She shook her head. "No need to stuff my face with somethin' fancy if I'm only going to puke it up later in a space suit. Assuming they even give me one."

Poor kiddo. I reckon she'd had a rough enough life without folks doggin' on her. I ordered my own grub and carried the tray of food to a table tucked back in a corner. My toes tapped beneath the table, bumpin' Mel's every now and again. She sipped the soup, which smelled of iron and hydroponics. I hated ship food and already missed the promise of Bay-zar's. It didn't take me long to devour my protein bar, all the while my eyes doin' a 360 'round the mostly empty room.

Mel's spoon was halfway to her lips with the last of the soup when the rest of them passengers arrived. Large clumps of 'em gathered near the door where they peered in at us like they was waitin' for her to turn *ryddarl* and kill 'em all.

Starin' at 'em, I almost missed the stranger. A shadow crossed over the table, and I growled.

Looked like time had run out.

3

Planet Miral

When the young woman's fingers combed through Mel's loose hair, I thought Mel would leap up or somethin'. But she musta seen the shadow cross the table 'cause she sat there cool as a...carrot. (*I think that's the word.*) In fact, she returned her spoon to the bowl, rested her hands in her lap, and waited.

If it'd been me, I'd a been unsettled by some stranger touchin' on my hair, assumin' I had any. I opened my mouth to say somethin' when the woman's mate joined her at our table. The woman's hands trembled as she spoke. "She looks weird with all this thick hair, but she could almost be our Jarra back home."

At the doorway, grumbles passed through tight lips, and a few folks braved my growl long enough to trickle inside. The couple didn't hurt on Mel, just played with her hair a bit before returnin' to their own seats. I caught Mel wipin' away a tear when she thought I weren't lookin'.

"You growled. I've never heard a *Tersic* growl before." She stared at her empty bowl.

"I expected trouble. You still hungry or somethin'?"

More passengers found reason to take up a seat in the mess hall. Weren't mealtime yet, but already the room was more full than I seen it the entire trip to Bay-zar. Mel shook her head, but I knew better. The way she eyed the empty bowl, she was still hungry.

I ain't seen a *hu*-man up close and personal-like, but I seen plenty of holograms and 2D photos. She weren't nothin' but skin and bones, all edges and elbows rather than curves. Nothin' like them images showed. "They be lettin' us off port-side whenever we reach some planet or another. You got a plan? I know ya said ya sorta lived on Bay-zar, though I don't know how one does that, seein's how it's nothin' but booth after booth."

My throat itched. All that perfume some of the passengers had been wearin' made my noses itch somethin' fierce, yet I weren't 'bout to leave Mel all alone. Not even to walk the twenty feet to the drink dispenser. She stared at her empty bowl and said, "I've been on Bay-zar for two years, moving from place to place until yet another town kicked me out."

"Where'd ya sleep?"

"Back of booths, rooftops, wherever I could."

Several folks 'round us grumbled in response. "And where did you live before that?"

There be all sorts a ways to respond to a question like that, especially when surrounded by a room full of strangers who want nothin' more than to string ya up and let ya rot in space. But I'll be damned if she did any-a-that. Mel straightened her shoulders as she told it, though she kept her eyes on that empty bowl like it were a beacon.

24

"My parents brought me to Bay-zar when I was six, back before the war really got going. They told me I'd love Bay-zar. All the bright colors and dangling pretties for me to watch, toys to play with as they shopped, and sweets to keep me happy. Sounded like a dream to me, really."

The couple from earlier nodded in agreement. I didn't recall much in the way of "pretties" in Bay-zar, but then, my vacation had been cut kinda short.

"When the *ryddarl* attacked, people blamed it on my parents. Said the *ryddarl* attacked because my parents were human and 'everyone knows humans are harbingers of trouble.'"

"As they are!"

The shout came from the mess hall's rear and half-a-dozen voices shushed it. Another voiced whispered the word *albatross*. "I didn't know any better. I was six, Eerl. What could I possibly know of politics?"

"*Tersic* don't hold the same prejudices as most folks," I said, and she ripped her gaze from the empty bowl. "So Earth sided with the *ryddarl* when the struggle began. So what? We *Tersic* didn't do much better. We were all set to side with 'em, too, when them *ryddarl* double-crossed planet Earth."

Someone dropped a cup nearby, and its clatter echoed through the silent mess hall. The corners of Mel's mouth tilted up in the first *gen-u-ine* smile I seen from her since Bay-zar. "Thank you," she whispered.

"Now don't go a-thinkin' that *Tersic* are all perfect or nothin'. We might not care where folks are from, but if there's one thing we can't stand, it's a liar." I'd been waitin' to see what reaction my words would bring. If she'd been lyin' to me, things were gonna get a mite complicated, but her eyes never left my face as she nodded.

25

I ain't expected much else from a youngin' like her, but it weren't just me she had to convince. Marta cleared her throat, and I flinched. My roamin' eyes had missed the two sisters' entrance. She and her sister rocked back on their mech-tails at the table beside us. "If the *ryddarl* killed your parents, how'd you survive?"

Between the time Marta cleared her throat and asked her question, someone done set another bowl of soup in front of Mel. My own mug of Aych-Two-Oh had been refilled. Unnerved me that someone got that close, and I ain't even notice. That there was twice.

Mel slurped another spoonful before answerin'. "My mom had been holding me at a booth with sparkling horns while my dad had looked into a part for the cruiser. He'd paid our way to Bay-zar by filling in for a ship's mechanic. At least, that's what I remember. The *ryddarl* ship had followed our leaking thruster trail to Bay-zar, but it wasn't my dad's fault. He'd told the captain it was dangerous to fly with so much damage, but the damned fool refused to listen. He'd wanted to make a buck and packing the ship full of passengers was the best way to do it. Getting them to Bay-zar meant getting paid. The *ryddarl* ship landed not ten feet away, and when my mom saw it, she shoved me under a booth table. Told me to be quiet."

As Mel talked, the faces of them passengers softened. Her voice, thin as silk, betrayed her fear to us, yet she didn't cry or shake or nothin'. It weren't the first time she'd told this tale.

"When the screaming started, I clamped my hands over my ears and curled up into a ball until the ground stopped shaking. By then, bodies filled Bay-zar."

"And yer parents?" I asked.

"Dead? Gone? I don't know."

"No way those folks on Bay-zar would raise a human." Angry words from behind us meant to stab—

26

but Mel shrugged. I turned my rear eyes to find Zee leanin' against the wall behind us. His Unified Military fatigues were rumpled and dusty like he'd been traipsin' through Bay-zar's black market, and his hat were missin', yet he still managed to look like a twenty-five gun salute on a Sunday as he glared at Mel.

Foolish girl glared back. "I didn't stay on Bay-zar. Someone found me, someone in the Unified Military. Told me my parents were dead. I'd hardly had time to process it when I was shipped off to an orphanage on Miral."

I shuddered. Miral was a hot mess when it weren't summer. Desert world orbitin' two suns and packed with miles of sand. And if the heat weren't bad enough, the planet was used by the UM to hold prisoners of war and the like. "That ain't no place to be raisin' kids," I said. Several folks muttered in agreement.

"Have you ever been to Miral?" she asked no one in particular. Not-a-one-a them passengers answered her, but they didn't hafta. The way their eyes avoided our table was answer enough. Mel slid up the side of her shirt and exposed a welt that stretched from hip to just below her brassiere line. Thing was as wide as three of my fingers and puffy. "Miral isn't an orphanage. It's a slave ring. *Ryddarl* sold prisoners of war to the Miral work camps, which included children. The Unified Military did the same."

"You lie!" Zee lunged at Mel, his face too bright a red for the rough blue fatigues. Her soup bowl hopped closer to the table's edge. Half a dozen folks pulled the law man off our table and held him back as he snatched for her. Zee hollered, "Let me go!"

Don't exactly know when the captain'd joined us in the mess hall, but there he was, holdin' onto Zee's shoulder. Captain spun him 'round and knocked him against the wall. "Leave this room. Now."

27

"I don't think so. That thing you're all defending is a liar and a thief. I'm not about to let her get away with it."

"Ain't ya on vacation, lawman?" I asked, and his face got all ugly.

"Walk away, *Tersic*." He tapped the stripes on his shirt pocket. "Vacation or not, I'm not about to let a lying thief go. And if you were half a *Tersic*, you wouldn't either."

Mel stood. Though her shoulders trembled, she stepped in front of Zee and rolled up the sleeves of her tee-shirt. A serial number was branded into her pale shoulder. Weren't puffy or nothin' like somethin' new either. You could tell that tattoo had been there a long while.

Her other arm bore lash marks—probly from some kinda whip—and when Zee ain't moved one inch, she raised the back of her shirt. More whip marks than healthy skin, all up and down her backside. I didn't wanna know what the rest of her body looked like.

"Call me a liar again." Though she whispered, everyone heard it.

Zee shook free of the captain. His singular nose, giant as it was, scootched up his ugly face with his grimace. "Screw you," he shouted before stridin' outta the mess hall in a huff.

People settled back into their seats, the captain among 'em. "Sorry about that. Zee's got a bit of a temper, like most in the UM, I suppose."

Mel shook her head. "Don't sweat it. I'm used to it."

"You shouldn't be!" I shouted and then winced at my brashness. "You done nothin' to 'im, yet he's set on treatin' ya like shit on his boots."

Marta and Barta squirmed along with a few others who'd been most vocal 'bout tossin' Mel out the air lock. It was good—they *should* be ashamed.

The captain leaned closer to Mel. "So how'd you escape Miral?"

He caught her with her spoon halfway to her mouth. I woulda sworn people were holdin' their breath waitin' for her to finish the story. When she'd eaten a few bites, she cleared her throat. "They made us mine on Miral. Hard work. Keeps us hidden since it's mostly underground. I saw a few people escape when the big freighter-lines came in to pick up raw materials. I just waited for my turn and hitched a ride out of there."

"You were a stowaway. But none of them were heading to Bay-zar—" Mel raised an eyebrow and the captain said, "No ships from Miral land on Bay-zar. Planetary leaders won't deal in slavery. So how'd you get there?"

"Captain, let her tell it," someone called out 'cross the mess hall.

Another few spoonfuls of soup and a swallow of tea someone had provided. "Bay-zar's one of the largest importers in raw materials anywhere in the galaxy. It's why all of you guys were visiting as tourists. A good quarter of the freighters leaving Miral's slave mines go to Bay-zar. The craftspeople there use the raw materials to make all that space junk tourists love." Mel pointed at the pin on Barta's chest. Weren't but a tiny little pin the size of a beetle, but it lit up in neon colors every few seconds. "Your pin tells the world you visited Bay-zar's Grand Market, but it tells someone like me, someone who's worked the mines, that it's made of iron with bits of silver thrown in so the crafter can charge more. It tells me you've visited Bay-zar, which takes ships from everywhere."

"He told me it was special silver! The thief!" Barta picked at the pin.

Always curious, that was me. I couldn't help it. "Yeah, but why'd ya go back to Bay-zar? I mean, what's there for ya now?"

Mel set the spoon in her now empty bowl. When someone offered to refill it, she gave a brief shake of her head. "Answers. The truth maybe. The UM told me what they wanted me to know and nothing more, but what happened to my parents? Did they really die? Were they taken by the *ryddarl* as slaves? What happened that day?"

"I can get that information from the databanks at port," said the captain.

She stared at the captain, her mouth hangin' open. "You'd do that? For me? Why?"

The captain shrugged. "Seems like you could use the answers."

"Besides, it'll irritate the hell outta that UM grunt, won't it, Captain?" He tried not to grin, but I seen his eyes twinklin' at the truth of my words.

"I...I didn't know that information was easily available."

"It isn't, but I'm a captain. I have access to—" The captain stopped, his eyes stuck on the doorway to the mess hall. A hundred bodies—at least them without eyes on the backs of their head—turned as one to scope out the disturbance.

Zee was back, a rolled-up screen clutched between his grimy fingers. When he reached our table, he shoved the flimsy object in the captain's face. His eyes moved 'cross text too far away for me to read. Mel tilted her chin up like she was tryin' to read it, too, but from the frown she wore, I'd bet she couldn't see it no-more than I could.

30

We didn't hafta wait long. The empty bowl clattered when the captain struck the table with his fist. The gaze he done turned on Zee was enough to melt suns.

"Mel, you'll take Rhiohl's old room. He's got no use for it now, and you'll need somewhere to sleep until we reach our destination."

"And what *is* our destination, Captain?" I asked.

The captain glared at Zee. "Miral."

Mel weren't goin' back there. No way in hell was I gonna allow that. I ain't never been to Miral myself, but lookin' at the scars on her body, no one need live through that. She didn't look much like no fighter, tiny little thing that she was, but the steel in her blue eyes spoke volumes 'bout her thoughts on the matter. As did the stiffenin' of her shoulders as she stared down the captain. She didn't hafta to say nothin' either. Them other passengers on *The Marzipan* near rioted at the captain's words.

"You can't send her back there!"

"What kind of man are you to send a child back to a prison camp?"

"Might as well let the *ryddarl* kill her now if you're sending her back."

The mere volume of their shouts was enough that them with sensitive ears clapped hands over 'em to shut out the sound. Seein' such a shift in those folks amazed me, I'll be frank. They weren't all kum-blay-de-da with Earthlings or nothin', but at least they wasn't seein' Mel as a threat no-more.

Zee didn't stick 'round either. Bet he knew what I did—had he stayed, there was gonna be a riot and him in the middle of it. Even with him gone, a riot weren't outta the question.

The captain held up a hand for silence. It took a minute for folks to settle, but they did. "Look, this is an

31

order from the Unified Military for me to drop Mel off at Miral. I can't go against the law, guys. I'm sorry."

More shouts and cries filled the mess hall. I turned to see how Mel was takin' all the chaos, but she was gone.

4

Zee's a Right Jerk

The corridor that ran the ship's length was empty. Mel ain't never been on *The Marzipan*, at least not that I knew. Weren't but a few places for her to go. She certainly didn't know where Rhiohl's quarters were located. A ship this size was too big to just go-a-guessin' on yer destination. I took a stab at her goal and set out toward my quarters.

When I got there, she was huddled outside my door with her arms wrapped 'round her knees. Her eyes were leakin' a bit, and she sniffed. "I didn't know where Rhiohl's room was."

"I figgered as much. Want me to show ya?" I stuck my hand out, and she used it to pull herself to standin'. "If ya look at the wall, you'll see colored lines."

She followed my finger and nodded. "Green leads to the mess hall."

"That's right," I said. "Green for grub."

Mel grinned. "I figured it was green because leafy vegetables are green."

"Veg-tables? Are those tables? Or is it more fish?"

"Fish?"

I pointed at her shirt. Before I could ask, she pointed at the red line. "Where's this lead?"

"Red's for emergency. Goes to the escape pods."

We walked down the corridor, and I gestured at another set of lines. "Blue and purple go to passenger quarters, the purple bein' the rich folks with them fancy suites. Lines work on each level. We're on level three now, but Rhiohl's room's on level five, so we gotta get down the stairs twice before we'll be on the right floor."

The lights embedded in the metal floor dimmed, signifyin' the shift to evenin' hours, and we passed several crew members in the stairwell. "Where are they going?" Mel asked.

"They're on their way to shift change. The dimmin' lights means its grub time, though I figger we cheated on that a bit."

Down two sets of stairs and we followed the blue line to the end of a hall where a door stood open. I ushered her in to find the room had already been cleared out. Mel peered 'round at the tiny room and almost head-butted me when she stepped back. "Sorry," she said. "Where do you think they put his stuff?"

"Don't rightly know. Probly boxed it for the furnace."

"Won't his family want it?"

I shrugged. "Too expensive to ship interstellar to return his junk to his home world. I doubt the captain's got dough to spend on that sorta thing."

Mel kicked off her boots and stretched out 'cross the wall-mounted cot in the corner. Weren't no chairs in her room, just the bed, a few shelves for holdin' clothes and the like, and a small table beside the cot.

"The toilet and sink are tucked into the wall," I said, slidin' 'em both out.

"Where's the shower?"

"It's a dry shower. Here." I pulled the accordion tube from the wall and pressed the button. A short blast of powder filled the air. I hated them powder showers—smelled like overly sweet perfume—but when travelin' in a ship with tight quarters, I could see why ship engineers opted for 'em.

Mel's nose crinkled as she inhaled. "Roses. I hate roses," she said.

"Roses. Flowers?" She nodded. "Ain't them. More likely one of them hybrid—um—hybridalecton plants from one world or 'nother. Or a weird combo of several. Never can tell. One ship, I'd swear it was hydraulic-oil scented."

A light laugh escaped her, and she glanced 'round. Her room was the size of my closet, but it weren't like she'd be stayin' long. As if readin' my thoughts, she leaned back against the cot's lone pillow, her eyes misty. "I won't go back. I don't care what that jerk thinks."

"Don't worry. I ain't fixin' to let 'em take ya back. Not by a long shot."

Mel closed her eyes at this. "Thanks, Eerl. I think I'd like to be alone for a bit if you don't mind."

She tossed her arm 'cross her face, but not before I seen the mask of strength crumble. I let myself outta her room and a moment later, she'd locked the door. Not that I blamed her.

All them folks changin' their minds and still, all's it took was one jerk to ruin her chance at answers.

I'd be damned if I was gonna let that happen.

Come mornin', I could hear them passengers mutterin's and gasps before I'd done left my room.

At first, I didn't wanna leave. What had transpired durin' the eve? Had Mel gotten into some sorta trouble? Or had that Zee done somethin' foolish? *Tersic* aren't exactly known for bravery, but our curiosity was gonna kill us as easily as that cat they're always talkin' 'bout. Before I could change my mind, I stepped into the corridor.

Marta and Barta were whisperin' as they passed by and a whole string of people followed 'em. "What's happened?" I asked.

"Go see for yourself," a stranger answered.

I followed the trail of passengers bein' shooed away by fidgetin' crew members 'til I reached the fifth level. Toward the hall's end, the captain's shiny head bobbed above the rest of the dawdlers. I spotted Mel's brown mess o' curls next and rushed to her side. Then I caught a glimpse of what everyone was starin' at.

The door to her room was shut, and bright red symbols had been cast 'cross the front of it. Weren't blood—if it had been, my noses woulda known—but it weren't exactly paint neither. Dirtier. Rougher.

The captain brushed a hand 'cross one letter, and it didn't smear none at all. The letters were in Common and legible enough to be read from a distance.

Estithia.

Common for a particular foreigner—one who carries a cursed soul. 'Twas one of the worst words that existed in Common as far as I knew. Mel stared at them letters like if she focused hard 'nough, they'd uproot themselves and change to some other word. "Who did this?" I asked.

She shrugged. "Does it matter?" Her fists were clenched at her side. "I thought after yesterday…."

36

"You thought maybe folks would be willin' to think on ya different-like."

She nodded. "Should've figured that people don't change. Once marked, always marked."

I flinched at the bitterness in her voice. "Captain, what's to be done?"

"About what?"

I threw my hands up at the entryway. "This! Someone is set on hurtin' Mel anyways they can. You gonna let a rat like this stay on yer ship?"

Mel placed a hand on my arm, and the heat drained from my face. "Don't, Eerl. Let it be. It isn't the captain's fault someone decided to redecorate his ship."

"Screw Zee," muttered the captain.

Mel stared at him. "But you'll lose *The Marzipan!*"

"It's *my* ship. I'll be hanged if I'm going to let him tell me what to do. We have to stop before Miral anyway to refuel. I'm going to look up those answers for you then. You deserve that much."

"Why?"

The captain blinked and rested a hand against the derogatory word. "Someone damaged *my* ship while trying to hurt one of *my* passengers. Besides, you remind me of someone."

He set off with a quick-like stride, and Mel tilted her head. At my nod, we trailed alongside him to the mess hall. Majority of the passengers were eatin' their breakfasts when we strode in. Mouths stopped chewin' at sight of the captain, and they ceased all their yappin' when they spotted us. The captain's shoulders tried to kiss his jowls, and his fingers clenched into fists as he sought and found Zee.

Those sittin' near the law man vacated their stools as the captain approached. "Get up!"

Zee spooned a lump of salty-smellin' mush into his mouth and stared at the captain. He swallowed before bitin' into a piece of dry toast. "Do you need something, Captain?"

"Get up, I said."

When Zee continued eatin' his grub, the captain grabbed hold of Zee's jacket collar and gave it a tug. Zee ain't even twitched, but he turned his head toward the rest of us. People in the mess hall had inched forward to form a circle 'round the captain and Zee.

"Don't even think about it, folks." Zee patted the firearm strapped near his rib cage. "This here's between the captain and me."

No one backed up a single step, though I was tempted to. I ain't comfortable 'round weapons. Mel leaned closer to me, her hand findin' mine to give it a squeeze. When he'd finished another bite of toast, Zee rose. He towered over the captain by several inches, but that didn't matter a lick as the captain raised his chin and glared right back.

"I take it you've changed your mind about following orders." The captain nodded, and Zee *tsked*. "Those were orders from the Unified Military. Refusal can and will mean the loss of your ship, Captain. I don't think you want that, now do you?"

"This is my ship. As long as it's mine, I'm in command, Commander Zee. If you want to tell me what to do, you're going to need more than the three stripes on your uniform."

"I've got connections aplenty, Captain. I'll have your ship seized for harboring a war criminal before you've even shit out your breakfast."

"War criminal? How does that work? She was all but five when war broke out."

"Section II, Article 3, Paragraph 10 of the Melhorn Proclamation states that all humans are property of the Unified Military for their role in the War of Terra-

Firma, to be reinstated as workers on Miral or Garna III...."

Zee rattled on at length 'bout a bunch of fancy documents like they mattered much out here in space. I waited for folks to jump in as they had before, but the mess hall held its collective breath.

The captain picked up his comm. "Set course for the nearest non-UM port."

"Roger that," the pilot answered.

"She'll get off port with me, Captain. I'll hire someone from there to take us to Miral. That is, after I'm done filing charges against you and your crew for failure to comply with a military operation," said Zee. When he pressed his snout of a nose against the captain's, both flushed with anger. "She doesn't need to search for her parents. No *estithia* has parents."

"So it *was* you who marked up the door on my ship."

Several folks gasped, and the piss and wind left Zee as he stepped back. "I haven't done shit. Not yet, I haven't."

People gave Zee wide berth as he strode from the mess hall for the second time in twenty-four hours, but he'd be back.

And when he was, we'd be in more than a mite of trouble.

All of us.

5

Gettin' Answers

The closer we got to port, the edgier Mel grew. I figgered a tour of the ship might take her mind off everything. That is, until a group gone and interrupted things. One moment we was enjoyin' the greenhouse, and the next, Zee, with several members of *The Marzipan*'s own security team, rushed through them glass doors. The Captain followed quick on their heels, and when he spotted Mel, his shoulders sank. "I'm sorry, Mel. I did what I could."

"What's goin' on, Captain?" I asked, but I weren't stupid. I knew what them men had come to do.

Mel's hand lingered on a bushy purple leaf beside her for a moment, and then she thrust both hands out in front of her. Zee slapped a bindin' coil 'round her wrists without hesitation.

"Wait! Where are ya takin' her?" I asked. Zee brushed past me, his shoulder knockin' me in the jaw. Mel followed behind him like one of the lost.

"Captain, ya can't just abandon her to that military nut! He'll lock her up 'til he gets her to Miral, supposin' she even survives that long!"

"What else can I do?" the captain asked, and he ran a hand 'cross his hairless head.

"You were willin' to stand up to him before. What's changed?"

"This." Zee dangled another screen before me, but he yanked it away before I could read more than a smatterin' of words. "I'm in control of *The Marzipan* now."

"And what law lets ya do that? Some Martial Law of Space or some shit? When did the Unified Military get the right to take ships away from hard-workin' folks over some *hu*-man?"

I'd gone too far. Zee's fist knocked me in one nose, and I crumbled like the sissy I was. I wished I could say I done passed out or somethin'. Might've made it easier to explain how I let that bully bind me as well, but I ain't got a reason other than bein' afeared of him. His heavy steps marched behind us as he goaded us to the lone cell for prisoners on *The Marzipan*.

Four steel walls that ain't been used for much else than storage is what that cell was. Several boxes were piled in the corner, but it was otherwise clean. Mel and me both tumbled in with a hard shove. Zee didn't waste no time tyin' me to the wall, before settin' Mel down on a wobbly chair. The way he stared at her, his mouth curled up too far at the corners, made my skin wanna leap up and hide under somethin'. I'd heard some pretty unsavory tales 'bout the Unified Military, but I ain't wanna believe 'em 'til now.

"Why were you *really* on Bay-zar? And don't give me any shit story like the one I walked in on in the mess hall," he said, and she smiled. Amidst all this danger, she found the bravery to smile at him. He repeated the question, and when she continued her bright beam, he done slapped her 'cross the face. You could tell she was used to it, the way she rolled with the force of his hand.

"Mel, maybe it'd be better to tell him. Maybe iffen he knew, he'd understand why we're so keen on helpin' ya."

Zee glared at me when I spoke. Mel held out her shackled wrists. "Undo the coil first. Then I'll tell you."

The way he tilted his head, he was doin' some right hard thinkin' just then, but I ain't seen why. Mel ain't but five foot nothin' and a hundred pounds with all them clothes on. Her boots musta been ten pounds of that. She weren't a threat. Zee musta come to the same conclusion as he undid the coil. "If you get up from that chair, I'll knock your ass out cold," he said and waved his fist at her. "Now, Bay-zar—why were you there?"

"I wanted to know what happened to my parents." Mel's lip trembled, and I stretched as far as my restraints would allow to pat her shoulder.

"I heard the end of that lie in the mess hall," said Zee. He held the coil up and gave it a shake. "Try again."

"It's the truth. You came in halfway through. If you want your answers, let me answer."

Just as in the mess hall, her story came rollin' out with little interruption. I'd heard it before—weren't nothin' to speak on at this point, but Zee—I expected him to grill her somethin' fierce. I mean, that's what an interrogation's supposed to be, right? Only he did nothin' of the sort. He gave it a listen, his brows furrowed 'cross that broad forehead.

When Mel finished, she peeked up at him with those wide eyes, but he weren't payin' her no mind.

43

Instead, Zee stared off at nothin' in particular. "Commander?" she asked.

"I knew your parents."

I musta misheard him, so I stuck my pinky in my ear to free up any wax. Finger came back clean. "What? How?" asked Mel.

"When the *ryddarl* attacked, your parents were trying to help some that got injured."

"Some of the folks on Bay-zar?" I asked and immediately wished I'd kept my mouth shut when Zee's lip curled in disgust.

"No, shithead. They were trying to help some injured *ryddarl.*"

Mel managed a half-rise from that chair when Zee knocked her back into it with a shove. "You lie," she hissed, and somethin' feral lit up them blue eyes.

He picked up the stone necklace 'round her neck. "I should've recognized this."

She snatched the stone from him. "Don't touch it again."

"Your parents said it didn't matter that they were *ryddarl*, they were injured. They needed saving. Here we were at war with the *ryddarl*, and the damned fools were trying to *save* them. Who the hell does that?"

"You must mean somebody else. My parents weren't traitors."

Zee reached into his pocket and pulled out a small bit of Mel's hair. I had no idea when he'd cut it from her, but it was creepy lookin' at him holdin' a piece of her so casual-like. He dangled it in front of her like a piece of meat or somethin'. "I ran this through the computer last night. Had to be sure," he said and handed her the chunk of hair. She rubbed the dark strands between her fingers.

He pulled a second piece outta the same rumpled pocket. This one was lighter than the first and a mite

44

finer. She musta recognized it 'cause she gasped. "I got this off you when you were just a child. The day of the attack. I wanted to remember who it was that—" Zee swallowed hard. "—That cost me everything."

Her chin was red from where he'd hit her, but her hands stayed put in her lap. Quiet-like and calm. I wanted to shout at Zee, to make 'im answer the million questions been runnin' through my brain, but I done none of that. I tried to stay still like Mel.

She broke the silence for me. "What did I do to you? Is that why you hate me?" When he didn't answer, she whispered, "Did you kill my parents?"

"No, but I should've. I would've. There they were, saving the enemy. Had my gun on them when another *ryddarl* ship came burning out of the sky. When it crashed, debris scattered everywhere. Killed your parents on impact. It's how I got this—" Zee turned down the collar of his fatigues 'til his broad shoulder were exposed. A foot long scar snaked down the side of his neck, 'cross his collar bone, and straight to his shoulder.

Zee ain't seen it. He was too busy tellin' his side of the story to see Mel's fingers grippin' the chair's side in a stranglehold that turned her slim fingers white. Nor did he see the way those same little fingers moved into the pocket of her pants, but I did. I twisted sideways 'til the rope gave and draped my arm 'bout her shoulder like I was huggin' her. When she turned toward me, it weren't peace in her eyes.

I shook my head a smidge, and her lips hinted at a smile. "My parents wouldn't have helped the *ryddarl*. Those monsters destroyed our home, our planet. What reason would my parents have to help them?"

"I don't know, but when I saw you again in Bay-zar, I knew it was you. Same brown-haired human I

45

rescued, same stupid girl digging where she doesn't belong."

Mel's hand in her pocket musta relaxed as the lump inside it smoothed. "It was *you* who pulled me from beneath the rubble. The one who turned me over to the military."

Zee nodded, and the lump returned as she made a fist. He barely noticed this time when she done shrugged off my arm and stood from the chair. "It was you who turned me over to those...those military freaks who sent me to Miral."

When she pulled her hand from her pocket, somethin' small glinted in the overhead track light. "Sit down," Zee ordered, but Mel didn't move a muscle. What was in her hand? I couldn't see, but this wasn't gonna end well.

"If ya saved her, why are ya tryin' to kill her now?" I asked. "Don't make a lick-a-sense."

"The *ryddarl* followed her parents' ship from Earth."

The commander was lyin' as plain as I was standin' there, and I fought to keep the grimace from my face. "Yes, but why hate *Mel?* I get yer hatred for her parents, but she weren't more than a gleam in the galaxy durin' all this. Ain't her fault the *ryddarl* followed them folks."

When he yanked me up by my square collar, my knees quaked. This military man was big—bigger than me and bigger than Mel. Weren't no way to take him on. Then I caught the light glintin' off whatever Mel held in her hand. She stepped forward a single step. Zee dropped me, and I near collapsed on the cell's metal floor.

"My partner," he hissed, and spittle hit Mel 'cross the cheek. "While I was so busy trying to save your parents and then you, the *ryddarl* were beating the hell

46

out of my partner. She was holding off a *ryddarl* a mile away. Saving you kept me from saving her."

Still didn't make no sense to me, but who was I to argue with a crazy man with a big iron on his hip. The thrusters shifted, along with the pressure in the ship. We were comin' up to port. Had to be with the change in direction and speed. Zee grabbed Mel by her hair, his eyes on fire.

Mel rested a hand 'cross his cheek. "I'm sorry for your loss."

When she done said that, I thought then and there he'd kill her. But the sorrow on her face broke my heart. Zee froze.

The Marzipan brushed against somethin' as it docked, and the impact knocked us off kilter. When Zee fell to his knees, I caught sight of that metallic, glinty-thing in Mel's hand. Some sorta shiv made from a fork or spoon. I couldn't rightly tell.

The minute she met my gaze, that shiv popped right back inside her pocket. I did believe she was gonna kill the Commander.

I don't know what shocked me most—that she was capable of stabbin' someone or what came next. One moment it was the three of us, and the next, all them passengers spilled into the cell's open door. At least, them that could fit. The rest huddled in the hall. Every last one of 'em were armed to the teeth with silly things like pots and sticks.

Zee shifted his weight to stand when Marta knocked him over the head with her pan. The rest of the group joined in 'til the captain called for a cease fire. The commander was out when the captain unlocked my restraints. Marta tossed somethin' pebble like at Mel and winked, while her sister yelled, "Run!"

Five minutes later, we were off *The Marzipan* and hidin' in the mass of crowds spillin' into the port at

Apasia. I coulda cheered 'cept we were abandoned and broke, with only a shiv between us.

And I still didn't know what a fish was.

6

We Need a Ship

In quiet contrast to Bay-zar, the port-side market of Apasia rolled 'cross several hills. Lotsa tents or shack-like booths—but none of 'em bumped up against each other like too many crates in a cargo hold. They was spread out easy like and castin' deep shadows as they blocked most of the sun. Weren't none too keen on bein' neighbor-like as they gave each other the wicked-eye.

Weren't but three tourists pokin' their heads in and outta one booth when Mel and I stepped off *The Marzipan*. That captain waited just long enough for us to clear the hatch before he was off, leavin' us in the dust and dryness of whatever town we'd ended up in.

It weren't the dust that left Mel's eyes red and puffy, and she dabbed at her eyes with the sleeve of her hoodie. My skin itched—like eyes crawlin' 'cross me or somethin'—and even though I took a gander 'round with all four eyes, there weren't nothin' to see. Just a lot of old folks shufflin' 'round their goods while hollerin' at two buyers.

"Mel," I whispered.

49

She flinched at the break in the silence. "What?"

I draped an arm 'round her and used the motion to toss her hood up. Without speakin', I steered her into an alleyway tucked between the Port Marshall's and somethin' called a "Super-Deluge Plantastical."

"Wait, where are we going?"

I shushed her and continued to tug her in the direction of a nearby overhang. Several crates and barrels rested beneath the shade. When I pulled her behind them crates, she wrested her arm away.

"What's wrong?" That chin of hers untucked itself and thrust upwards in defiance. It was a look my momma woulda whipped outta me in a heartbeat had she seen anythin' like that, but on Mel, it was…well, Mel. She weren't 'bout to let no-one tell her what to do or where to go, but she ain't seen the danger.

I jabbed a finger back in the direction we come from, and her lips formed a small circle as one of them "tourists" ducked into our alley. His nosy self poked 'round a bit, and seein' nothin', he wandered back port side.

"When we landed, there was three of them tourists shoppin' 'round. *The Marzipan* took off and the minute yer face was visible, one of them up and disappeared right quick-like. I ain't seen where he skedaddled, but them other ones was givin' ya the eye. We're too visible on this planet," I said.

She pulled the corners of her hoodie closer and sighed. "You think Zee was tellin' the truth?"

"Hard to say. We ain't seen his test results. For all we know, that snippet of hair were fake. Could've been from a dog or lethra or somethin'. Only one way to find out though. We need access to a computer."

Mel nodded. "I doubt this town's got much, but they should have a central computer. Somethin' hooked up to Galactalnet."

50

I didn't feel like pointin' out the obvious, but if there was any truth to be had from Zee's story, we needed to keep things nice and quiet-like. I'd lay down money if I'd had any that he'd sent out an alert on Mel the moment he'd had her identity. If this town had access to the 'net, chances were the law 'round here woulda seen 'em.

"Stay here," I said and eased out from our boxy cover. Instead of hangin' back the way we'd come, I followed the alley to the other side where it dumped me in the middle of some sorta town square. Biggest buildin' before me was some sandstone mess they called an inn, but next to it stood a wooden shack that had to have seen better days. It stood mostly straight, though solely through sheer stubbornness or maybe someone's prayers. The sign overhead called it a Library Center.

Books were somethin' I knew. You could call me a collector of 'em if ya were so inclined. Most folks didn't like the dust that came with haulin' 'round a several hundred-year-old stack of paper, but there was somethin' 'bout the smell of 'em that I liked. You could tell a story from those smells—where the book had been, who'd held it, even what tree it had come from. Or ya could iffen ya had my noses. Figured a town this dusty wouldn't notice the extra dust bunnies, which musta been why they had themselves a *gen-u-ine* library.

When I got back to Mel, she was tryin' too hard not to sniffle and them eyes were a smidge redder than when I'd left her. "I found us a library," I said, and she near knocked her head on a crate when she stood.

"How'd a backwater town like this end up with a library?"

"Don't know, but I reckon they have 'net access. Gettin' in may be trouble."

"Why?" she asked. "More townsfolk?"

51

I shook my head. "You. You look too *hu*-man."

Mel grinned and dropped to a crouch. Her fingers tucked into the sides of her combat boots where she fished for somethin'. When she pulled it out, I bit off a chuckle. In her palm she held a round microchip which she smacked against her forehead. The chip curved and rippled for a second before it popped out like a spare belly button, only this one blinked. Now this little *hu*-man was sportin' a third eye on her forehead. The blinkin' were a bit sporadic, but so long as no one looked too closely, she'd be all right.

Or so I hoped.

"Where'd ya get one of them thingamajigs?"

That smile again. "Marta. Tossed it to me before we ran."

"Smart Marta," I whispered. As we come up on the alley's exit, a tumbleweed rolled 'cross the town square and bumped against a dry fountain. A little kid tossed a coin inside where it glinted in the sun.

"Stupid kid," Mel whispered, and I cocked an eyebrow. "Damned fountain's empty. Wishes only come true if the coin's submerged in water."

"Why's that?"

"Coins tossed in feed the water mites. No water, no water mites. No water mites, no wishes."

Made a mad sorta sense, I reckon. There was so much I could learn from Mel 'bout the *hu*-mans. If only we could find her folks so she could put this all behind her. She followed me up the Library Center's creakin' steps and through the propped open door.

No sunlight inside—only e-lamps encased in this thick, insulated glass. A man hunched over on his stool where he guarded a second set of doors leadin' to the library proper. His unibrow twitched at our entrance, but otherwise he continued readin' whatever displayed 'cross his tablet.

When he pointedly ignored us, I tapped the top of his rickety desk. He glared at my finger 'til I removed it. "If you're done poking at my desk, what do you want?"

His voice reminded me of dried paper. Dried, old, and long dead paper. Beside me, Mel's third eye blinked at him as she grinned. "I told my Pa they'd have a proper library here, but he said ya'll ain't nothin' but a backwater hole fulla nothin'."

If she hadn't stepped on my foot, I mighta gasped at her imitation of my accent rather than rollin' with it. As it was, I was hard pressed not to laugh when she turned them gleamin' teeth on the poor fool. He stood up and straightened his shoulders in response, then turned to me. "I'll have you know, sir, that we are the largest collection of printed texts this side of the galaxy."

I doubted it, but who was I to argue? I raised my hands. "Iffen ya say so."

"Now, Pa, don't insult the man," Mel whispered a touch too loud, and the proprietor straightened his polka-dotted bowtie.

"Are you looking for anything in particular, miss?"

Mel shook her head. "I've always had a hunkerin' to see real *gen-u-ine* books. All them trees cut down just so folks can see them fancy words written in real ink. I heard once long ago they wrote with feathers. I wasn't even aware chickens and such made ink!"

His eyes narrowed. "Chickens? What are chickens, miss?"

My hands clenched in my pockets, but I had no reason to worry. Mel grinned before she answered, and his stiff shoulders relaxed. "I read it once. In some book. This critter had feathers, and them crazy *hu*-mans used to pluck 'em and write with them feathers or somethin'."

"Ah! Yes, chickens. A fowl of some sort from Earth, I believe." Mel nodded. "Well, no chickens here, miss, but you are welcome to peruse our books." The man pressed a button, and the second set of doors opened with a gust of stale air. No dust—just the smell of ancient things ticklin' my noses.

The outside weren't nothin' to cough at, but they'd spared no expense makin' sure them books were well-protected. The glass casin's were so tight, I only sniffed the hint of trees. Everything else were blocked out.

I went in first and set one eye to searchin' for a computer. One dilapidated machine sat in the corner near a square glass case. The little man shuffled in behind us. "You can use the computer there to call up any book we have. The Bot will retrieve the book for your perusal inside the case."

Mel stuck out her bottom lip. "Ya mean I won't be able to hold them books?"

"No, ma'am!" he snapped. "Some of these books are seven hundred years old. One touch and they'd disintegrate beneath your fingertips. Now if you'll excuse me." The little man shuffled back through the second set of doors, which shut behind him with the slight hiss of hydraulics.

"That was risky," I whispered, but Mel ignored me. Her fingers already crawled 'cross the light-keys as she typed.

"Where'd you learn Common?" she asked as she scrolled through a list of records.

"School. *Tersic* are quite educated."

"No, I mean that *accent*."

"Books."

Mel covered her mouth with her hand. "Earth books? No wonder you've got such a—" Zero results came up in her search, and she scowled.

"Nah, ya ain't gonna find nothin' on Bay-zar. What ya want is the Unified Military computer system. Try lookin' up yer parents' names in the UM personnel database or checkin' the war's data logs."

She waved a hand at me and returned to typin'. Her search on Bay-zar turned up nothin', like the search before. With a grimace, she pulled up the military records. "Eerl, don't look," she said, and I frowned.

"Don't look at what?"

The barest hint of tears touched her eyelids. "I don't want you to see. Their names, I mean."

"Why?"

"B-because they're mine. Their names are all I have left. I don't want to sh-share them."

It made me nervous. I can't say why, only that it did, but seein' her so…vulnerable, I turned my back to the screen.

"Close your eyes."

I'd been hopin' she wouldn't notice. I shut my rear eyes as requested. All 'round me were books from a thousand worlds, most more valuable than *The Marzipan* and all her crew, and I didn't want none of it. All I could think 'bout was that damned fish, and Mel sittin' here wonderin' if her folks were dead or not.

When she made a little chokin' sound, my skin itched somethin' fierce to see what she'd found. Mel tugged my elbow.

"What?"

The second tug made me open my eyes, but I weren't gonna look at that screen 'til she said. "Eerl…please, I changed my mind. They—"

Her words drew my front eyes to the screen where two folks stared back at me. Two faces held Mel's button nose and her brown curls, though the man's was shorn much shorter than I'd expected after seein'

55

Mel's waist length hair. I'd expected to see the words DECEASED stamped next to their names, but the word weren't there.

Instead, the computer read:

> NAME: O'Brian, Pat *(& Mary)*
> DOB: 02/18/2604
> LAST SEEN: *Ryddar*
> Prisoners of war wanted by the Unified Military.
> Reward of 150,000 credits upon return to a UM controlled port or planet for sentencing.
>
> ALSO WANTED: Mel O'Brian
> LAST SEEN: Bay-zar

The record rattled on with facts 'bout Mel and her family. Seein' her folks names like that held a certain power. I mean, her folks mighta still been out there. Assumin' they escaped that *Ryddarl* ship's crash. "Here ya been searchin' for answers, and ya done found the whole-kitten-caboodle."

"Kit-and-caboodle," she said with another wave of her hand. "They're alive, Eerl. My parents are alive."

"Maybe."

She spun in her chair, her long braid smackin' me in the thigh. "What do you mean maybe?" Mel jabbed a finger at the screen. "It says right there—they're on *Ryddar*."

"A lot of *hu*-mans were taken to *Ryddar*. Prisoners of war, as the screen says, Mel. Most were killed or enslaved. Even if yer folks made it there, *Ryddar* ain't a pretty place. There's no guarantee that yer folks are still alive."

Mel slammed a fist into her thigh. "But they could be!"

"Only one way to find out."

In the screen's reflection, her eyes widened, and she clutched the stone danglin' at her neck. "Is…is that even possible?"

"For you, yes. You're *hu*-man. They'd kill me on sight, but if we had a way to sneak in or somethin', maybe we could find out if there's any truth to the record."

"Why did Zee lie?" Mel cleared the screen with a wave of her hand. Behind me the second door opened, and the little man poked his head in. "Let's go."

As we approached the doors, the man's cheek twitched as he eyed Mel. His gaze landed on her third eye and stayed there. He didn't say nothin' to us as we left, just watched warily. As we passed through the front doors, that same "tourist" stood lookin' down at the empty fountain outside. The minute I seen him, I pulled Mel 'round the corner of the buildin'. We leaned 'gainst the side, and when the stairs creaked, I held my breath.

To my right, Mel crept 'long the wall, one foot at a time. She'd already near reached the buildin's rear when the "tourist" said somethin' to the library proprietor. Only took one word for me to follow Mel to the shadow of the alley.

"We gotta find somewhere to hole up 'til we can get us a plan."

"I've got one," she whispered. I almost stopped mid-stride when she said it, but no tellin' where our shadow was. Once we'd ducked back behind our hidey crates, I opened my mouth to ask, but she pressed a finger to my lips. "Stay here."

"Wait—what?"

Mel took off runnin' down the alley, too fast for the likes of me to keep up. Even if I used my rear leg to propel me forward, she was faster than a speedin' pellet. One moment I could see her, and the next, she'd darted off some direction or 'nother. Whatever she was up to, I couldn't see what good was gonna come of it.

If I were lucky, she'd be back shortly, and we could figger out what was what. If luck had abandoned me, as it seemed to have done most of this vacation, she'd be snatched, and I'd be sittin' here waitin' for someone who ain't never gonna return.

I settled into a crouch on my third leg and waited. And waited. And then I took bets with myself on whether I'd ever see Mel again.

I won.

7

I Found Us a Ship

When the crickets chirped and the temperature bellied out, I gave up waitin' behind them crates. I stretched and peered out into the shadows when I seen someone movin' up ahead. Limpin'. Until I saw a bit of braid stickin' outta her hood, I thought it was maybe our mystery tourist.

As Mel got closer, a splatter of blood painted her boots and the bottom of her jeans. I'd moved out from beneath the shadows before I'd done thought it through, but no one trailed behind her. Not that I'd blame 'em—somethin' scary lurked in her eyes as she limped back to me.

She ain't seen me, even when she stood less than a foot from me. I touched her shoulder, and she stopped mid-step. "Get-off-of-m—" She paused, her eyes busy focusin'. "Eerl."

"You smell of blood and fear. What happened?" I tried pullin' her back toward the crates, but she shook her head. "We need to be less visible."

"No, this way. I found us a ship."

"Mel, wait," I said, rushin' to catch up with her. Even with a limp, she was truckin' it 'cross the alley like hell itself was on her tail. It was surely on mine as I followed. What was with the blood? How'd she gotten us a ship with nothin' more than a shiv? I shivered, and it had nothin' to do with the settin' sun neither.

She led me through a maze of streets, every one of 'em empty. Once I caught sight of someone standin' on a porch, but they ducked back inside with a hiss and a door slam. Another alleyway, and there it was.

A small speeder.

Wasn't the best ship for long range, but it would get us to *Ryddar*, assumin' it had enough fuel and workin' parts. I'd never set foot in a ship that small, but I supposed there was always a first time for everything.

The hatch opened with the slide of a battered ident card, and my brows twitched. When no one greeted us inside, my brows danced with my forehead. "Mel," I said, grabbin' hold of her arm. "Wait a second, what's going on? Whose ship is this? How'd ya get 'em to agree—"

"There wasn't any agreement." She sneaked a peek at her shoes before steppin' into the ship's bow. The hatch closed, and I stood there, one chump up shit creek.

By the time I'd gotten feelin' back in my extremities, the ship was already airborne. Mel was alone in the cockpit. And she was pilotin' the ship.

"Put it on auto-pilot."

She flinched at the growl in my voice. "Can't. Not until we're free of the gravitational pull."

"See, how do ya know somethin' like that? When did ya learn to pilot a ship?"

I slid 'cross the cockpit and grabbed hold of an overhead grip as we done pulled further away from the

60

planet. My skin felt oddly light for a mite before it settled into its rightful place. We were free of the grav. She slapped a button with the butt of her hand, and the computer beeped in response. "Have a seat, Eerl," she said, wavin' a hand at the stool beside her.

"I'd rather stand."

"You aren't standing. You're leaning. And it's driving me nuts. Please, Eerl, sit."

A dryin' droplet of blood gave her shirt's fish a double-dotted i. Mel caught me starin' at it and rubbed her hand over the spot. It smeared 'cross the w. I didn't wanna sit. Truth be told, I wanted to run, but there weren't no-where to run. Besides, with the look she been givin' me, I'd been a fool not to listen. The backless stool creaked beneath my weight.

"This here's a *Gandey* ship."

Mel sighed. "How'd you know?"

I pointed at the stool. "No backs."

"So? It's a stool."

She spun on hers and for a moment, I could almost believe her to be the youngin' she'd been back on Bay-zar, the little girl who was gonna tell me what a fish was and why it didn't need a *bi*-cycle. But only for a moment. When she stopped her spinnin', the smear of blood reminded me of them dead bodies back on Bay-zar when the *ryddarl* attacked. "You're *hu*-man, so ya think like a *hu*-man. Like a bipedal creature. *Gandeys* have three legs, like me. Can't sit in a backed-chair. Where would yer third leg go?"

"It could have been any tripedal creature," she said, but I shook my head.

"Not with a cushion this thick. Tender rears, them *Gandey*. But you're changin' the subject. How'd ya get the ship?"

"Eerl, before you get mad—" This was gonna be a whopper. I could feel it in my chest. "—the Gandey

61

was already dead when I got there. No corpse was going to need a ship like this…."

She musta seen the wince'cause her words trailed off. "Mel, start at the beginnin' and tell me all of it. Be truthful like now."

One of the lights on the control panel lit up like a galaxy. She gave it a glance before she spun to face me. "I was looking for someone I heard about." I opened my mouth, but she held up a hand to stop me. "Eerl, when I was on Miral, I had to grow up fast. Either that, or I was gonna be just another dead body left for the sun to strip of flesh. You don't know what it's like there."

Mel stared at nothin', her eyes doin' this sorta shifty thing between me and the air. She remained like that, all silent-like 'til I nudged her with my foot. "I've seen pics. Ain't nothin' like bein' there, I suppose, but I wasn't born yesterday. I know a few things 'bout slavery. Earthlings weren't the only folks tortured durin' the war."

"I-I didn't know that." She swallowed hard. "If I wanted to escape, I needed skills. All those humans there, it was easy to find a pilot. I made him teach me how to fly."

"How? I mean, there're hundreds of ship types out there."

"I know. All we had was this burned out husk of a *Gandey* ship. The kids used to hide in it sometimes when the—well, when things were rough."

"And ya just so happened to find a ship like that back there?"

Another light lit up, and this one she checked with a lever. Our speed accelerated, but I only knew that by the number on the screen. Artificial grav were workin' a sweet spell for a ship this small. Neither of us bothered strappin' into the harness that lowered 'cross

62

our shoulders from overhead. "When we left *The Marzipan*, I saw the *Gandey* ship land in the distance. I knew it was around, so I went in search of it. Found it not too far from the library. When I knocked on a nearby hut, no one answered. The door just opened on its own—" Her lips scrunched up at my frown. "No, really, it did! A-and when I walked in, the *Gandey* was sprawled out dead. He hadn't been dead long—he was still warm."

"You sure he was dead?"

She shrugged. "He wasn't moving."

"Did ya check his pulse?" When she shook her head, I added, "Did ya get down on the floor and check his breathin'? Nothin'?"

"Eerl—he was pale green—" A siren above the dash blared to life, and Mel's hands danced 'cross them controls. "—He wasn't breathing, he had no pulse. No need to check. If a *Gandey's* gone green, they're dead. And we will be too if you don't stop staring at me and let me concentrate."

Pilotin' a ship was never somethin' I'd picked up. Never had the need bein' a homebody. Truth is, the trip to Bay-zar'd been my first vacation off-world. Been short of two weeks and already I'd seen more than I had my entire life.

Whatever was wrong with the ship didn't look like much. No shakin' or vibratin' where it shouldn't, no steam or fumes pourin' out into the halls, and no sudden drop or rise in temperature. But Mel gripped the yoke like our lives depended on it, her brow a sweaty sheen in the panel lights.

One moment I was concentratin' on not breathin' too loud, and the next, we were passin' through the glow of an interstellar gate.

That small ship quivered like Marta and Barta when they first seen Mel, and I seized the handhold for the ten ticks required to pass on through.

The harsh glow disappeared, leavin' me starin' at the bluest planet I ever did see. Oceans filled the view screen, marred only by a dozen archipelagos of land. Waitin' for her to speak was the longest five minutes of my life, I reckon. And when she did, I almost choked on my own spit.

"*Ryddar.*"

"What?"

"It's *Ryddar.*"

I leaned closer to the view screen, even though I knew better. From this distance, them specks of land told me nothin' 'bout nothin'. I tapped the screen with my finger. "It's too blue. *Ryddar*'s all burned out and such. Weren't supposed to be nothin' left after the war."

Mel pulled up a map overlay on the screen. "This is what it looked like before."

The picture she showed held land. Entire continents even. Nothin' like that remained now—just a trickle of islands here and there and maybe a larger hunk of land the size of a small country back home. "Even still, the way I heard folks tell it, this place was almost in cinders when the war ended. That's clean air down there—clean water, too."

"Only one way to find out," she whispered. Before I could do more than let loose with a loud hoot, the ship was planet bound.

This stolen ship was swallowed whole by blues. Incredible seein' a sky that clear, much less all that water. And while it soothed me, my eyes twitched. If we were lucky, the planet would be the shell it was purported to be. We'd find nothin' and leave. If Lady

Lucky didn't smile down on us, we'd find *ryddarl* waitin' instead.

Lots of 'em.

How Mel stayed that calm on the outside I'd never know. But then, she'd been full of surprises. Whether the ship's owner had been dead or not, weren't no reason to steal his ship. What if he'd had kin? Ya never knew the reasons for a person's belongin's, what needs they have or don't have no-more. When I noticed my foot tappin' and Mel's eye roll, I settled my nerves as best I could.

Which is to say I took a breath and clenched my eyes shut for a time. I waited for the communicator to buzz or somethin' as we broke through the atmosphere. Nothin' but radio silence greeted us.

"Where ya gonna land?" I asked.

She pointed at one of the biggest islands—this one shaped like a lengthy squiggle. "Computer reads a fair number of heat signatures in that region. Whatever or whoever lives here, probably lives there."

"Nothin' on the smaller islands?"

Mel shook her head. "Not anything large enough to register as intelligent life, at least not by this ship."

I'll give her this much—girl was smart. She didn't plop down in the middle of town or nothin' the way I woulda done. She set our stolen ship just outside civilization near the brush. The landin' thump near drove my teeth through my lip.

When I followed her lead, she turned and gave me a slight frown. "Are we cool?"

I tilted my head. "I don't follow."

"Are we cool? OK? Bueno? I-I don't want you thinking any less of me for taking that man's ship."

We weren't "cool," but what could I say? She was my ride outta this joint, and I weren't 'bout to mess that up. So I simply nodded.

65

Her face relaxed into a smile. "Good. You've been really nice through all this, defending me against Zee and the rest of the passengers. I just wanted to say that I appreciate it, Eerl."

The lump in my throat done doubled, but I managed to spit out, "No problem. Always root for the wonderfrog, my momma liked to say."

"Underdog."

"What?"

"Nothing." She left the cockpit first. I paused at the doorway, my eyes caught by the glint of steel. "You coming?" she called without lookin' over her shoulder.

I snatched the small pistol from the net shelf and tucked it in a pants pocket. "Yeah, I'm right behind ya."

She reached the hatch but stopped before it opened. That same knife as before was in her hand as the other pressed an ident card against the lock screen. The door slid open. No one waited for us.

Mel exited first, her boots leavin' tracks in the moist soil below. My noses crinkled at the air. I woulda never thought clean air had a smell, but it did. A green, earthy smell like mud and rolled leaves and the hint of rain. Weren't a smell all that different from the islands of *Tersia*.

The soil sank beneath my three feet. A twig broke nearby, and we both jumped. A five-legged creature peered out at us from beneath the brush. It bleated once before tuckin' back into the shadows.

"Come on," Mel said as she set off in the direction of the heat sources.

I followed along for 'bout a quarter of a mile before I stopped. "Mel, wait."

"What?"

"What are ya gonna say to them folks? What are ya gonna do if they're *ryddarl?* We need a plan before we just bust in there all shelly-nelly."

"We have a plan." When I cocked my head, she held up her knife. "This is the plan."

I couldn't help but glance down at that blood on her pants and boots. "Was that the plan with the ship's owner?"

"I told you, Eerl, he was already dead."

"Then explain the blood."

"When I walked inside the hut, I tripped and fell. Landed in his blood."

It weren't the first time she'd seen blood. I don't know 'bout you, but if I'da tripped and fell all spread-parakeet into a puddle of blood, I'da been out the door screamin'. I wouldn't have stopped for anything, especially not no ship.

Her eyes glinted in the sunlight for a moment before they returned to their vulnerable state. "Please Eerl, just trust me. I know what I'm doing."

And that was the problem. She really did.

8

Ryddar

Them history books will lie to ya, boys and girls, and they'll do it every time. The small settlement we stepped into weren't abandoned, and it weren't full of decayin' folks long leftover from no war neither. No one was outside to greet us or nothin', but smoke and the hint of some sorta stew pulled me toward one of the ten buildings.

"Where are you going?" Mel asked.

I pointed a finger at the closest buildin'. "Someone's makin' grub in there. I can smell it."

Mel placed a hand on my arm. "Me first."

She held the knife in front of her, her fingers vise-like 'round the hilt. Like that tiny butterknife was gonna protect her from a *ryddar*! I shoulda went first, but I'm a chicken through and through. Least she had a visible weapon. No need to use mine iffen it could be helped.

The door opened easy enough, but the front room were empty of occupants. A pot of somethin' lay cookin' in the fireplace, but no one was mindin' it as it tried to bubble over.

A door lay at the rear, and I jabbed my finger in its direction. "I reckon they be in there."

"Who?"

"The owners of this here hut."

A small cough from behind the door confirmed my suspicions. When Mel's hand touched the doorknob, the door swung open in a rush and hit her smack in the face. She tumbled back as somethin' with fuzzy hair swung crazy limbs in a mad dash for the door. I blocked the person's trajectory, and it came to an abrupt halt not more than a foot away.

Once he stopped movin', he stopped bein' a creature and showed himself to be *hu*-man. Two legs, two eyes, two arms, and one nose—just like Mel. His thinnin' hair stood up on end like a dustball, and his bare feet were coated in a fine layer of mud.

He took one look at me and screamed.

Mel stepped between us, her fingers grippin' that knife of hers like a savior. "Stop," she said, and his lips smacked shut.

"Who're you?" he mumbled.

"I'm…I came here to find my parents. Computer back on Apasia said they were last seen here. Who are you?"

The man stumbled back. "Oh my god…. You're Mel! Mel O'Brian." Her knife clattered to the floor. The man brushed past her on his dash out the door.

I didn't stop him. Somethin' told me not to, not this time. It only took her a minute to react, and then I was alone in a room where some stew was now burnin'. A cry went up outside, and I left the fire alone with its food.

For a time, I'd thought maybe we'd be findin' Mel's parents outside the way that man all up and knew Mel's name, but it weren't her folks. Bunch a *hu*-mans grouped together 'round the man with the bushy hair as he talked.

"Look at her! She looks just like Pat if ever there was a day."

An old woman, her hair the color of a sun, touched a wrinkled hand to Mel's cheek. Her backwards retreat sent Mel steppin' on my feet, and she spun, her hand still grippin' the blade.

"It's just me," I whispered. She tucked the knife in her pocket.

"We're ever so sorry to have startled you," said the old woman. "It's just, we were informed you were deceased, back on Bay-zar."

"How do you know that?"

Mel's words were venom, and I touched her shoulder. Them folks behind the old woman were edgy enough without addin' Mel's stress to the situation. "Mel here's been through some…trauma since Bay-zar. Maybe give her a peck of space and answer her question," I said, and the old woman nodded.

"My name is Frances," she said as she held out her hand to me. I shook it, as I'd done Mel's several days ago on Bay-zar. Frances's fingers were cold and soft—not rough like Mel's.

"I'm Eerl."

"A…*friend* of Mel's?"

I shrugged. "Met her on Bay-zar a few days ago. Been travelin' with her since."

Frances' brows furrowed for a time before she righted her sight on Mel. "I'm pleased to know you're alive, child. Your mother always swore you were."

"I-is my mom here?" Several folks shuffled off all silent-like, givin' me the answer to Mel's question. The

71

girl weren't stupid—she caught on almost as quick as I did, and her shoulders slumped forward. "She's dead, isn't she?"

"Is there somewhere's we can talk?" I asked, and Frances nodded.

The bushy haired man followed us to another house, this one little more than a lean-to patched together by random sheets of metal and spare ship glass. The inside weren't no better than the outside with the draft seepin' in through a dozen holes in the walls. "Before the war, this place held a thriving economy. The monsters, the war, left little to thrive."

I flinched at *monsters* and hesitated before takin' the offered seat on a stool in the corner. The other chairs in the lean-to were backed—chairs for *hu*-mans—but they creaked when their legs were stressed by weight. "Ya done lived here before the war?" I asked.

"It's…more complicated than that. How much do you remember about your childhood?" she asked Mel.

"You mean before Bay-zar?" The woman nodded. "Not much. I know I must have lived on Earth—there are fuzzy memories of our apartment there. I had a room and–and a teddy bear."

The thought of her huggin' a real live bear made me grin too wide, and the old woman peered at me through squintin' eyes. "Sorry, I had to remind myself them teddy bears ain't real."

Frances patted Mel on the hand, and this time, she didn't flinch at the contact. "I know we were on Bay-zar for vacation, but I don't remember much else."

"I'm not surprised. Your mother told us that you were barely six when your family took that trip. But where are my manners? Would you like something to drink? A snack to eat, or anything else we can provide?"

72

I shook my head despite my grumblin' stomach, but Mel nodded. When the woman shuffled into the back room, Mel dabbed at her eyes with the corner of her hoodie's sleeve. She caught me lookin' at her and pulled her hood closer 'bout her face. The silence remained 'til Frances came back carryin' a tray with some fancy drink in a ceramic pot and a plate full of round bread-things.

"Here, dear. Have a cookie," the old woman said. Mel nibbled at the edge of one while the woman poured some brown liquid from the pot. "Before the war, the *ryddarl* were similar to humans—they had families and homes and everything a people could want."

This time I couldn't help but laugh. "The *ryddarl* are nothin' like humans. At least, not based on my research."

"You study the *ryddarl*?" asked Frances.

Beside me, Mel stilled in her seat. "No, but everyone knows 'bout them monsters. I've made somethin' of a study of Earth and its people," I said.

"Is that why you keep asking me about fish?" Mel asked, and I grinned.

"Exactly. Gotta built up my knowledge somehow. You're the first *hu*-man I ever did meet after all. Back on *Tersia*, I was a *gen-u-ine* researcher of Earth."

No one laughed.

Mel brushed crumbs from her hoodie, and Frances continued. "Before the great war and long before my time, people traveled the stars in grand ships—grander and far superior than the one you two rode in on I'd imagine. These travelers colonized many systems. One was Earth and another was *Ryddar*."

The cookie slid from Mel's fingers.

I'd heard this garbage before, rumors 'bout common ancestors and all that. Apparently Mel had too; she stood, her hand in her pocket. "You're one of those Believers."

"Believers?" For all the tone was inquisitive, the question didn't reach the old woman's eyes.

"Yes, Believers. These crazy people who told tales at the war's beginning about how we needed to love the *ryddarl,* because they were the same as humans. Like we had some sort of connection to those monsters."

"We do."

She moved too fast for me. Mel's hand flew outta her pocket, but luckily, it weren't holdin' the knife. She slapped Frances 'cross her wrinkled cheek. "No. We don't."

"Mel," I said and tugged on her arm. "Let her finish her story."

The woman weren't shocked. She'd had this reaction on folks before. Frances gave a sad smile and said, "Thank you—"

I held up a hand to interrupt her. "—Don't go thankin' me yet, lady. I'm just along for the ride."

"Those monsters killed my—"

Frances cleared her throat. "But they didn't, child. Your parents lived here on *Ryddar.* They weren't struck down on Bay-zar."

"How'd they die, if ya don't mind my askin'?"

Mel's jaw clenched, but she kept her peace. "Few years ago now, Mel's mother broke her neck tumbling down a nearby cliff. Her father wasn't himself after that. Something in him grew still. One morning, he didn't wake up. Such is the way with some people."

"You act like living here was something they wanted, like it was a pleasant experience!" Mel knocked her cup to the floor where it rolled 'til it hit a table leg. "It was slavery, pure and simple."

The old woman sighed. "It was, yes. For a time anyway. During the war and even for a brief period

74

after, *Ryddar* was the rotting shell everyone says it was. Once the war had passed and the *ryddarl* fled, life settled down for us. We were free. Stranded, but free. We built our homes and lived our lives with our families. What more could you want?"

"*My* family. I didn't get to live with *my* family. The torture never ended, not until I killed—" Mel bit her bottom lip.

So I'd been right. She'd had to kill some slaver or somethin' to get off that hell-hole and catch her ride to Bay-zar. The story she'd told had been too easy. Fool girl had lied to me.

She peered at me from beneath her lashes. I tried to keep the calm on my face, but I must've failed as she shrank in on herself.

"I'm sorry for your suffering, Mel." Frances reached out to touch the girl again, but Mel flinched.

"Just tell your damned story."

Frances shot a glance my way, and I nodded. "There was one difference between the Earthlings and the *ryddarl*. Earth may have fought in many battles, but they never had the *Hur-göh*." Neither of us reacted to the word, so she continued her tale. "While Earthlings remained human, there was an evolutionary leap in the *ryddarl*. Most were a simple people, but others developed a lust for violence and mayhem. This sect splintered off to form the *Hur-göh*. They believed…differently from the *ryddarl*. Whereas the *ryddarl* sought peace and prosperity on this world, the *Hur-göh* were not appeased by such *simple* things."

"They wanted war," I said.

"Exactly. They wanted what they lacked so they learned to take. They believed in divide and conquer to a fault. It wasn't just a way of life for them. The *Hur-göh*'s very DNA changed. They possessed strength and speed the rest did not. Once they'd conquered everyone on *Ryddar* there was little else to do. They set out to loot and kill among the stars. You could say they abandoned *Ryddar* for greener pastures."

There was a knock, and the man from before poked his head inside. "I thought Mel might like this. Belonged to her folks."

He sauntered over to Mel and thrust the picture frame in her direction without lookin' at her. Her fingers shook as they caressed the jagged-wood frame. Mel's back was to me, but I didn't need more eyes to see she was cryin' and tryin' hard not to show it. The man dipped his head once before leavin'.

"Mel? You okay?" I asked.

The sleeves of her hoodie couldn't wipe away them reddened rims as she sought out her seat. She tilted the battered frame toward me. The picture were different from the computer on Apasia, but them folks were the same. Between 'em sat Mel—a much younger and naïve Mel. Lookin' at her child-self, I couldn't figger how I'da ever thought this older Mel innocent. My eyes fell to the blood on her boots.

"I-it's my parents."

I nodded. "Picture's much older than the computer one."

"This was taken on Earth. This was the day before we left for Bay-zar." Mel's eyes burned black holes in the photo. The wood creaked in her grasp. "Tell me who was after them."

Frances took a sip from her cup. "To understand who sought their deaths, you must first understand how they lived."

"Don't get all metaphorical or philosophical on me. Just tell me what I need to know, so I can find the *ryddarl* responsible."

At this point, Mel wasn't gonna listen to a lick of reason, so I rightly kept my mouth shut.

76

"Our society collapsed during the war," said Frances. "Earthlings. *Ryddarl.* We were all at fault—be it for starting the war or for plain choosing the wrong side. People blamed us."

"Or folks just wanted revenge," I added.

The cookie between Mel's fingers crumbled halfway to her mouth. "We?"

My skin grew warm. Listenin' to Frances, I'm come to suspect a few things, but apparently Mel hadn't caught on. "I was getting to that, honey," said Frances. She reached out to pat Mel's hand but stopped halfway. "Your parents returned here to escape the *Hur-göh.* Who would look for two separatists from the *Ryddar* government on their own homeworld?"

Mel shot up like a coil bound too tight in a ship's piston. "What did you say? *Their* homeworld? My parents are from Earth. *Earth!*" Frances's silence infuriated Mel further as she paced 'cross that small room, her hands balled into fists.

"The *ryddarl* aren't Earthlings," I said, my eyes pacin' with Mel. "You've obviously been on this planet a long while. Maybe too long?"

"If you reach far enough back, we share a common ancestor, Eerl. But I'm not claiming the *ryddarl* are from Earth. Mel, your parents were just like me. What do you see when you look at me?"

"A liar."

I bit back a retort, but Frances smiled. "Physically, what do you see?"

Mel's eyes crawled 'cross Frances. "You look human. Of course, I can't see if you've got a tail tucked beneath your clothes or anything."

Frances whistled a short little ditty. The man who'd brought Mel the picture frame returned. "Yes, Frances?" At Frances's beckon, he stepped forward 'til

77

he was 'bout a foot from us. Under the overhead light, his skin was darker, almost thicker lookin' than Mel's.

"My skin's mostly translucent. My veins are visible, see?" Frances held out her arms. "Go ahead, hold yours out."

For all she didn't wanna, Mel's arm jerked out beneath the flickerin' light. She shoved the sleeve of her hoodie up. That same thinness made her veins pop out like someone had drawn on her in blue marker. The man's arms bore a slight hint of blue near his wrists but nothin' more.

"Jesse was born on Earth. His parents were human," said Frances. I swallowed hard, and my hands got all sweaty. This weren't gonna end well. I scooted closer to Mel. "Our thin skin is part of our genetics. Part of the *ryddarl* trait."

Her knife moved, but I'd been ready. Mel's hand didn't make it but a foot before I knocked it outta her hand with my fist. "No, Mel. There's been enough killin' today."

She growled at me, her muscles tense as she crouched. "Those t-things killed—"

"But they didn't, did they?" I asked. "Yer parents were here the whole time."

"And why is that, Frances? If they were *ryddarl* bastards, why was I born on Earth? What were we doing on Earth to begin with?"

Jesse snatched Mel's knife from the floor, but he didn't make no move to return it. "They wanted a better life for you than this. With the *Hur-göh* set to obliterate our way of life and your mother expecting, they couldn't remain here. It was too dangerous for them, especially considering that your father was one of those most outspoken about the direction of capitol politics."

"You have an answer for everything, don't you?"

78

I shoulda been watchin' her better, but when I looked at Mel, I admit to seein' that dirty little kid on Bay-zar. Blood splashed 'cross the bottom half of her clothin' had changed things but not enough.

When she stepped toward Jesse, I thought she'd gone and tripped over a chair leg. But when she righted herself, that knife was in her hands and the sneer smeared 'cross her face carried too much Zee in it and not enough Mel.

Whoever Mel had been, whatever child I'd known, were gone.

9

The Truth

"They were human. Say it." The knife glittered in the flickerin' light. Our eyes followed its motion as Mel twisted it in her grip.

Frances shook her head. "But they weren't, child. No more than I am."

Mel lunged forward and pressed the blade against the old woman's throat. "I'm not *ryddarl!*"

Beside me, Jesse eased back a step, tryin' to edge his way to the door, but Mel snapped her fingers. "Don't go anywhere unless you want her blood splattered across the floor."

"Mel, stop." The moment I said them words, she flinched and dampness gathered along her eyelids. "You're better than this, Mel."

"No, I'm really not, Eerl. Now, *Fran*-cis, unless you want to bleed out, you're gonna revise your story and tell me how my parents died."

"I already have."

"You're lying. About the *ryddarl*, how they died, why—the whole stinking story."

Jesse had stopped movin', but he rummaged 'round in his pockets before comin' up empty handed. He shot Frances an apologetic glance. The old woman's shoulders slumped a bit as she sighed.

"Nothing you do to me could be any worse than I've already lived through under the *Hur-göh*. Your parents were *ryddarl*—" A thin line of red appeared at her neck. "—and they were proud of that. Just look at your necklace."

Mel's free hand clutched the round stone at her neck, and it pulsed at the warm contact.

"It's a rhoa-stone." This from Jesse who'd made it a whole step closer to the exit.

"A what?" I said.

"A rhoa-stone," said Frances. "They're native to *Ryddar*. The only stones I know of that react to body heat are rhoa-stones. They're an excellent heat source in an emergency, too. But that stone I'd recognize anywhere. Your grandmother passed it on to your mother when she married your father. Told them both it would bring them good fortune and luck."

Mel's face flushed, and the knife blade trembled against the ridges of the old woman's throat. Mel ripped away her necklace and tossed it to the ground where it cracked. The stone went all dead-like, its glow fadin' to nothin'.

"I-AM-NOT-*RYDDARL*."

I couldn't let her do it. She was gonna gut these folks like caribou, and it didn't set right with me. "Mel, please. What happened to the nice girl I met on Bay-zar?"

The blade left Frances's throat as Mel spun to face me. "Eerl, you're an idiot if you think I'm a nice girl. Surely you've figured that out by now."

I held one hand out for that blade, while the other settled in my pocket. She couldn't see where it rested or nothin', and that was my meanin'. Keep her eyes on me and off them folks. I was the one who done brought her to their home, and chicken though I might've been, I weren't 'bout to let her just off 'em or nothin'.

She saw my hand waverin' and grinned. Too much teeth again as her lips spread wide. "Don't think you can take me, Eerl. These fools are liars, and if there's one thing I've learned in my time being bounced around the galaxy, it's that liars can't be trusted."

No, they can't.

I didn't say it out loud or nothin'. Not yet. "Mel," I said, and the blade jabbed in my direction—a mild feint as her eyes were too wide and her jaw trembled. "Besides bein' curious, what's somethin' else ya know 'bout *Tersić*?"

She bit her lip and sniffed. "They don't hate."

When she smeared her sleeve 'cross her face, I relaxed my pocketed hand. "That's right. We don't abide by prejudice. Nor do we abide by liars, Mel. If I thought this woman was lyin' to hurt ya, she'd never leave this house."

Mel nodded. "So you understand why I have to do this."

"No, I don't reckon I do. Come on, let's just go."

"Not until I get what I came for."

Jesse had reached the door. The floor boards creaked as he leapt outside, all the while Mel was glarin' at me. She cursed and made to go after him, but I snagged her elbow as she passed. "Let me go, Eerl! Please, I don't want to hurt you."

83

She meant it. Probably the last honest thing she done said to me since she'd killed that man for his ship, maybe since before that. Hearin' her plead with me 'bout broke my resolve, but if there's one thing the *Tersic* can't stand, it's a liar.

And Mel had done lied a whole lot.

I tapped a finger to her chest, my finger tracin' the *f* on her shirt. "Mel, what's a fish?"

Her eyes rolled back as she snarled. "This again?"

"Yes, answer me, and we'll all walk away from this place. What's a fish?"

Outside, a stampede of feet and angry voices approached, and Mel glanced back and forth between the door and Frances. The old woman dabbed at her neck with a hanky and waited for us to decide her fate.

"Mel, what's a fish?"

She threw her hands in the air, and that knife dropped to the floor. "I don't fucking know, Eerl! I don't even know!"

My brow furrowed as I tilted my head. "But yer shirt—"

"Yeah, I know, it's on my shirt. A shirt I stole from some kid back on Bay-zar. Little jerk ganked some of my food when he thought I wasn't looking, so I snagged his clothes as he slept."

The way she said it made my skin crawl. Callous. Bitter. "Did ya kill him, Mel?"

"What? No. Why would you ask me that?"

"Why not? You done already killed that fool for his ship. Who knows how many folks ya done knocked off in yer attempt to get to yer folks. So now what? You're here. Yer folks are dead and gone. What now, Mel—"

"Stop!"

"What now?" I repeated, and she clamped her hands over her ears. The shouts of the crowd outside

84

doubled. They weren't happy folks neither. "You hear that? They're none too happy with ya right now."

She eyed the knife on the floor, then her eyes crawled back up to mine. "I—these *ryddarl*—dammit—"

"If ya kill Frances, ya become everything people says you was. A *hu*-man, a killer," I said.

"But if I don't…."

"Iffen ya don't, what? You're a *ryddarl*?" She nodded and a few tears sprinkled 'cross her cheeks. "Does it matter, Mel? You didn't care one lick what them folks on *The Marzipan* thought of ya. Why do ya give any care to what these folks think?"

Mel dragged her boot 'cross the floor and shut her eyes. "Eerl, please. Don't hate me, not you."

I tried to smile, to copy the way the corners of her lips used to turn up too far. My cheek muscles twitched with the unusual action. "I don't hate ya, Mel. I don't know ya."

"Get me out of here—just get me out," she whispered.

There she was. The young girl I'd met on Bay-zar.

She stood, small as night in that room, her stolen shirt tauntin' me with the unknown. "Okay, Mel. We'll go out the back."

My hand rested in my pocket, my grip damp. I motioned for Mel to go ahead of me, and we passed through some rear door and into a kitchen. The noisy crowd swelled, and I shut the door behind us. There weren't no rear exit, least not from here.

If only she was still the girl I done met on Bay-zar. If only she'd known 'bout fish.

If only she'd not been lyin' to me from minute one.

Mel didn't see the pistol I drew from my pocket, but her body tensed when its barrel done poked her in the small of her back.

85

I woulda thought she'd turn 'round and face me, be all defiant like she had with Zee and the captain, but her body done stopped, like she was tired of fightin' or somethin'. "Make it fast, okay?" she whispered.

"You aren't gonna ask why?"

The tip of a braid shook loose. "Nah, I know. Damned *Tersic*. Curious to a fault, and the most honest people in known space."

"Ya lied. Ya misled me."

"I did."

The crowd broke through the front door, and Frances cried out somethin' in *ryddarl*. Fists and feet pounded on the wood door behind me, and I watched the wood shake from the force. Mel choked back a sob, and I asked, "Do ya even know what a *bi*-cycle is?"

"No."

It was a frog-like croak that escaped. Not the strong words of a *hu*-man or those of a *ryddarl*. The door frame shook. Them folks were comin' up fast. My gun wavered between the door and Mel.

"It's a *ve*-hickle, I think." I licked my chapped lips. "Sad that ya ain't never seen one. I was gonna find me one in Bay-zar, and see if my momma was right." Behind us, wood splintered and I laid my eyes on that angry mob—all sticks and stones and proud anger. *Ryddarl*, like Mel here.

No, not like Mel. It weren't right to think of 'em as I had.

I pulled the trigger.

ACKNOLWEDGEMENTS

This novella was an accident. One moment I was planning the sequel to *Amaskan's Blood* and the next, I was writing what I thought was a short story. Before I knew it, it was a novella worth the interruption!

Writing this story was a risk. It's non-traditional sci-fi that delves into very dark places, but I've never been one to shy away from a topic because it made someone uncomfortable. We each carry the weight of our prejudices, and we're each capable of great and terrible things.

First and foremost I have to thank Connie Willis, Christopher Barzak, and the rest of the Locus Writers' Workshop for encouraging me to finish this story. My brain stressed over planning the sequel to *Amaskan's Blood* and keeping my deadlines, but your laughter at the opening scene gave me the necessary push to get it done.

Many thanks to Maia and David for your helpful and thorough critiques, and to my beta readers for once again providing feedback on plot holes, name spellings, and general snafus. Thanks to my editor, Mimi the "Grammar Chick," for your amazing eye that catches more than I ever would.

Special thanks goes to the original inspiration for "Mel." Your story is, if anything, more important because it occurred out here in the real world rather than in the pages of a book. Everyone carries their own prejudices and fears—something you taught me in a school hallway so long ago. You've never been afraid to be you, for which I am eternally grateful.

As always, thank you to my amazing husband who

supports everything I do and encourages me to do more.

And lastly, thank you to those who are reading & reviewing my books.

I do this for you.

ABOUT THE AUTHOR

 Raven Oak is the author of the fantasy novel, *Amaskan's Blood*, and the upcoming science fiction space opera, *The Eldest Silence*. She spent most of her K-12 education doodling stories and 500-page monstrosities that are forever locked away in a filing cabinet.

When she's not writing, she's getting her game on with tabletop and console games, indulging in cartography, or staring at the ocean. She lives in Seattle, WA with her husband, and their three kitties who enjoy lounging across the keyboard when writing deadlines approach.

Raven is currently at work on *Amaskan's War* and *The Eldest Traitor*.

Raven Oak can be found online at the following:

Website: http://www.ravenoak.net
Twitter: http://twitter.com/raven_oak
Facebook: http://facebook.com/authorroak
Goodreads: http://www.goodreads.com/raven_oak

Please enjoy a sample of Raven Oak's coming-of-age epic fantasy, *Amaskan's Blood*. Available worldwide in paperback and eBook!

The Forest of Alesta, in the Year of Boahim 235

She was thirsty.

Thirsty was an understatement. Her tongue felt thick beneath the sour cloth jammed in her mouth, and Iliana swallowed hard. Tree branches thick with leaves whipped her shoulders as they passed. She did her best to make herself small, invisible, if only so the big one would stop looking at her.

His eyes—pale blue moons set in skin so dark Iliana couldn't tell what was skin and what was fabric. All three Amaskans wore solid black from head to foot. No ornamentation or lacings. Just tight, black silk, bound at the waist and wrists.

The same black fabric that bound her wrists together.

The big one glanced over his shoulder as the horses galloped through the forest. They traveled as fast as the muddy terrain allowed, which wasn't fast enough as the big one shouted a lot and gestured—all stabbing fingers and waving hands. They spoke to one another in a strange language—but Iliana knew when they talked about her. They called her *moquesh.*

Bait.

Most of the words were foreign, but that one bore enough similarity to Alexandrian that she could guess the meaning.

Another tree branch slapped her, this time across the cheek, and she closed her eyes against more tears.

Why had her father sent her away? The big one peered over his shoulder again, and she shuddered. It didn't help that rain poured down overhead—hard enough that not even the trees' thick canopy could block it out.

Had she been allowed to talk, she would've asked for a cloak. Either way she'd probably still be wet. The gag left Iliana able to do little more than groan as they traveled. And to think. And cry. Iliana stuck her bottom lip out, which trembled as she sobbed against the black rag.

She hadn't *really* thought her father would send her away. Tears rolled down her cheeks to mix with thick raindrops. *Papa, why did you send me away?*

Something had been off.

First, there had been her father's unusual appearance in the playroom. When Iliana and Margaret had raced for him not even the nanny's lurch forward and stern remarks had protected him from the onslaught of childish arms and legs.

Second, he'd allowed it. They had clambered up his six-foot frame until he balanced one sister on each shoulder.

But the final clue had been his smile. Lines had gathered around his mouth and eyes—lines that multiplied every time another rock hit the side of the castle walls. But as her father had smiled at his twin daughters, his eyes had remained muted and distant.

One moment she was on her father's shoulder and the next, he had rushed through the castle passageways until he'd reached the stables. Uncle Goefrin had been waiting with the three Amaskans, one of which he had told Papa was his brother. That was the first Amaskan, who led their horses at the front of the line.

They didn't look like brothers. His nose wasn't big enough.

Iliana had screamed until they gagged her. Then she'd kicked with her booted feet, but she'd been tossed astride a monster of a horse so ugly and large, she'd clamped her mouth shut out of fear it would buck her. Hands bound to the pommel, they'd left her feet free in the stirrups. A swift kick had done nothing.

The horse had ignored her until one of the Amaskans, a female, had spoken to the gelding. Then the horse had moved forward at a canter. Her father had cried out to her, and Iliana had craned her head and seen Goefrin restraining her father by the shoulders as he shouted her name. Her father's face had crumbled, and he had hidden it behind his hands as the Amaskans took her away.

He had said it wasn't safe.

At first, she'd cried too hard to notice much more than a blur as they passed through the city, but as the small group reached the outer walls, blood painted the ground crimson and the cries of the dying left her mute astride her horse. Arrows and rocks flew overhead as they pelted the Alexandrian guards and bounced off stone walls. The clash of steel nearby frightened her, and when the female Amaskan slit the throat of a nearby enemy, Iliana huddled as close as she could to the saddle and shut her eyes tight.

They were already halfway through the forest when she gained the courage to open them, and that was only because her horse stopped. "If ya want to live, don't run. Understand?" the female asked. When Iliana nodded, the woman unbound her hands and lifted her from the horse. When the woman set Iliana down on the leaves below, she slid in the mud and fought for balance. The Amaskan—Shendra, her father had called her—pulled a black tunic and boy's breeches out of a bag and shoved them at Iliana. "Change into these."

Iliana tried to ask where, but the gag muffled the question. The woman must have figured it out as she only shrugged. "There's no one here but the four of us. Change now, or I'll do it for ya."

While the two men stood guard, Iliana tugged at the laces of her dress and tried not to cry. *Always be brave* were her mother's words earlier that morning, and Iliana bit her lip. The knots came loose, but she struggled to get the thick, layered fabric over her head. The hem, caked with mud, clung to her face and tangled in her arms. In a panic, she shouted into the gag. When the sound of ripping fabric reached her, she twisted and screamed louder.

"Stop it—hush," Shendra hissed as she hacked away at the dress's fabric. The ruffles of blue fell to the forest floor, and Iliana's green ribbon floated into a muddy puddle, more earth-colored now than moss. Iliana's cheeks flushed while goose pimples pricked her bare skin. She tugged the tunic over her head and the Amaskan helped her buckle the breeches. Before Iliana could grab the ribbon from the mud, Shendra plopped her back on the horse and bound her hands to the pommel.

The trail of horses continued their gallop until darkness made it impossible to see, and by then, Iliana's teeth chattered and her stomach rumbled. The big one watched her until Shendra stepped between them. The woman removed Iliana's gag and unbound her hands. Iliana tried to swallow, but her mouth was too parched. "Here," the woman said, and she held up her canister of water.

Iliana coughed on the first swallow. The water only reminded her of her hunger, but she dared not speak. The look in the man's eyes kept her silent as they set up a campfire. Only a droplet or three from an overhead leaf remained of the earlier rain, but Iliana huddled against her horse for warmth as her clothes were soaked through.

"Here, make yourself useful." Shendra tossed a brush at Iliana, and its coarse bristles poked her hands when she caught it. Iliana stared at the horse in front of her.

She couldn't brush all of him. She couldn't even reach his forearms. Shendra whispered something in Sadain, and the horse lay down. Iliana touched the brush to his back and giggled as he squirmed beneath it with a whinny. The brush caught on specks of mud and blood; the latter Iliana tried not to think about. A good ten minutes left the horse much cleaner and drier than before. When the beast stood, mud and leaves from the forest floor stuck to his underside and legs.

The big one spoke, the sound just behind her, and Iliana spun around to find him looming over her. He held a dagger in his hands, and she screamed before falling to her knees. The shadow over her shifted, and Shendra knocked the dagger from the big one's hands. "What's this now?" asked Shendra.

His grin left Iliana shuddering. "We have our orders."

"Yes, to bring her to Bredych."

The man shifted on his feet, and Shendra matched his movements. "Someone hasn't been given the full plan," he murmured. "No matter, I'll see my part of the job done."

A leaf crackled behind Shendra as the second man approached, but the woman didn't move. Fear drove Iliana to the other side of her horse where she peeked through the gelding's legs. "What in Thirteen Hells are you blatherin' about? The job was to get the girl, take her back to Bredych for ransom."

"Not quite. Bredych's orders are to kill her."

"I don't believe ya—I know you're fairly new to the Order—Sayus, is it?—but Amaskans don't kill children. We aren't Tribor."

Iliana cried as she clung to the horse's leg. Her tears distracted the man, and in one heartbeat, Shendra moved. One moment she stood several lengths away and the next, she hovered over the man with her blade against his neck. He chuckled as he held out a piece of parchment, which she seized with her empty hand. "Damn," she whispered.

"Looks like you don't know Bredych as well as you thought," muttered the second man from behind Shendra. He held his blade against her neck, though his arm shook and a whisper of blood appeared.

"That's my brother you're talking about. He wouldn't order this. He couldn't," shouted Shendra, and the birds in the trees overhead cawed in protest.

Iliana crouched down and slapped her hands over her ears. She didn't see when the body dropped, but heard the thud as it landed in the soft soil.

One of the men uttered a groan and then a pop as his lungs filled with blood. The second man fell after a scrape of blades and a few grunts. The squelching sound of boots in the mud approached, and Iliana clamped her eyes shut harder.

When Shendra touched Iliana's shoulder, she screamed. Iliana didn't stop screaming until Shendra shook her. "Hush," the woman whispered. "I won't hurt ya."

Iliana pointed at the dead bodies. "I don't b-believe you."

The woman pointed at the mark on her jaw. "Do ya see this mark? Do ya know what it means?"

"It means you're Amaskan."

"Yes, it does. Amaskans serve Anur, God of Justice. Have ya done evil?"

Iliana wrapped her arms around her shoulders. "I took my sister's ribbon." Her favorite. The green one.

"That's not evil. Would it serve Anur to kill ya?"

"N-no, I guess not. But you killed—"

"Amaskans don't kill children." Shendra picked up the forgotten brush and set about picking the mud out of the horse's hair. Iliana backed far away from the killer and leaned against a hollowed out tree trunk. The wet wood seeped into her already wet clothes. When a beetle climbed across her arm, she jumped.

She wanted to go home.

A howl from the trees sent her stumbling back toward the woman with the sword, killer or no, and Iliana watched the woman finish removing the mud from her horse before moving to the next. "Go sit at the fire if you're wet."

Iliana's jaw ached, but she stood by the woman's side. "I-I'm fine."

Shendra paused mid-stroke. "You're cold. Go warm up." When Iliana refused, Shendra asked, "What? Why won't ya go sit by the fire?"

"If that–that Bredych wants me dead, who cares if I'm cold?"

The hug was unexpected, and Iliana flinched at the contact. "No one's gonna kill ya. I promise. On my life to Anur, I swear," Shendra whispered.

Iliana touched a grubby finger to the tattoo across Shendra's jaw. She'd expected it to feel rough somehow, scratchy, but the black circle was smooth to the touch.

"As long as you promise..." she whispered. Iliana peered out into the night made darker by the forest trees and shivered.

Stay up to date on future releases from the author by **Joining the Conspiracy**, Raven Oak's official mailing list. Get sneak peeks, exclusives, freebies, & more.*

Visit **http://www.ravenoak.net** to sign up!

Word of mouth is the number one **best** way to ensure that your favorite authors have continued success—better than any paid advertisement.

If you enjoyed this book, please consider leaving a **review** on Amazon, Barnes & Noble, Goodreads, and other retail or reviewer sites.

Your review is greatly appreciated.

CPSIA information can be obtained
at www.ICGtesting.com
Printed in the USA
FSOW04n1332300817
38183FS